SUMMER
PROMISE

SUMMER PROMISE

AMISH SEASONS
BOOK 1

Marianne Ellis

JOVE
New York

A JOVE BOOK
Published by Berkley
An imprint of Penguin Random House LLC
penguinrandomhouse.com

ISBN: 9780593334881

Berkley hardcover edition / August 2013
Jove mass-market edition / July 2021

Printed in the United States of America
1   3   5   7   9   10   8   6   4   2

One

Miriam Brennemann stood at her kitchen window, gazing out toward the green fields beyond. It was a still summer morning in early July, the color just beginning to creep along the edges of the sky. The air carried a chill, and the floor of the big farmhouse kitchen was cool beneath Miriam's bare feet, but she had been up at this hour often enough to recognize the promise of the day: It would warm up soon enough, turning hot and fine.

Oh, Daed, she thought. *This is just the kind of day you always loved.*

On an ordinary day, Miriam would be bustling about the kitchen, preparing the breakfast that she and her husband, Daniel, would share when he came in from feeding the livestock in the barn. Miriam's father, Jacob Lapp, would come from his section of the house, the *dawdi-haus*, to join them. The three would talk over the work for that day, drinking the *kaffi* Miriam always made strong and dark, eating the hearty breakfast all would need for the long hours of work ahead.

Then Daniel would head to the fields while Miriam and Jacob walked to the end of the long, straight drive that led from the farmhouse to the main road. There, they worked together to ready the family farm stand for that day's business.

But everything was different now. Jacob Lapp had died three days earlier, passing quietly in his sleep, a simple and straightforward relinquishing of earthly life and a moving on to his new life, with God. Today he would be laid to rest beside Miriam's mother, Edna, the wife who died of a fever so long ago. There were many who would come to honor her father, Miriam knew, for Jacob had been both well respected and well loved among his Plain and *Englisch* neighbors alike. But the one who would come the farthest was Miriam's younger sister, Sarah.

Sarah. Sarah is coming home!

Miriam tried to picture the sister she hadn't seen in four and a half years. The image was faint but the emotions were vivid.

It was ridiculous to feel so unsettled, Miriam told herself. Sarah was her sister, after all. Unlike others Miriam knew who had made the decision to leave the Plain life, Sarah had not stayed close by. Instead, she had made a home for herself in faraway San Francisco, first at the university, where she had gotten her degree, and now in her first job.

She'd sent a letter every week of the six years she had been gone. Collections of her thoughts and impressions, glimpses of what happened during the day, jotted down before she went to bed each night. It had always seemed to Miriam that reading one of Sarah's letters was just the same as listening to her sister talk. Miriam had discovered them, stacked by year and tied with pieces of household twine, in the bottom drawer of her father's chest of drawers. She knew her father treasured the letters. He had saved every single one. Clearly they were precious to him.

All of a sudden, Miriam spun away from the sink, marching with determination to the kitchen door. She thrust her bare feet into the plastic clogs waiting there and took down a key that hung on a hook by the door. She opened the door, stepped outside, and shut it behind her with a quick snap, as if she feared that she might yet change her mind. And then she was moving, her quick strides eating up the yard. Not until she heard the crunch of the gravel driveway beneath her feet did Miriam slow her pace.

Sarah. Sarah is coming home today for our father's funeral.

She had come back to Lancaster just twice, both visits early in her time away.

It was easier for me that way, Miriam admitted to herself as she topped the rise of the small hill that lay between the farmhouse and the main road. Was that a bad thing? It was not that she had ever wished for Sarah to leave—or stay away. Only that once she had gone, things seemed simpler. Simpler with Daniel, Miriam thought. The hard knot of doubt that she had held in her chest for years seemed to loosen a little when Sarah was gone.

Miriam paused for a moment, gazing down. She could see her destination now: the Stony Field Farm Stand. Just seeing the stand comforted Miriam. It was her *daed*'s place and hers as well. Even more than the house where she'd been raised, the farm stand brought her father back to her.

Miriam started down the hill, picking up her pace until she was almost running. *Ach*, but it felt so good to move! To be doing something, even if all that "something" involved was a walk. As was the Plain way, since her father's death, neither Miriam nor her husband had been responsible for any of their usual chores. Instead, friends and neighbors had come to help get ready for the funeral. They had taken over all the daily tasks that went into keeping a farm going so that Miriam and Daniel had time to mourn together. But in truth, when Jacob's body had been prepared for burial by the *Englisch* funeral home in town and then returned to the farmhouse, Miriam had spent many hours sitting beside her father alone. She prayed silently, giving thanks for Jacob's life. On the outside, she appeared calm. But on the inside, her thoughts scurried back and forth, no matter how hard she tried to capture them and make them move in their usual orderly lines.

Daed was dead, and everything had changed. But there would be even more changes to come. Sarah was coming home. Not just for a few weeks, but for the rest of the summer, her longest stay since leaving six years before. Just thinking about it made Miriam's stomach hurt, and the fact that she felt badly about this made it hurt even more. She *loved* Sarah, and worrying about what might happen as a result of her visit did no good. It did no good at all. What would happen did not rest in Miriam's hands. It was in the hands of God.

Miriam reached the farm stand, using the key she'd brought with her to open the padlock on the back door. She opened the door and took a step into the building. Her fingers moved toward the light switch, then paused. *I didn't come to see,* she thought. *I came to feel.* Certain of her footing, for she knew every inch of this place by heart, Miriam took several more steps forward. Though Miriam was far from fanciful, it seemed to her that she could almost feel the farm stand reach out to envelop her.

It smelled so good! But the way the farm stand smelled was never the same twice, Miriam thought. It changed with the seasons, just like the goods her father sold. Could this be why it reminded her so much of him? she wondered. Her father was like this place that he had created, solid and sturdy on the outside. But inside, he still had the ability to surprise. He had certainly surprised everyone by giving Sarah his blessing to go off to college.

Help me, Daed, Miriam thought. *Help me to be like you, to accept with grace what I cannot change.*

And that was it, Miriam thought. The true reason that her stomach hurt at the thought of Sarah coming home and staying for so long. Miriam would have no choice now. She would have to face the fear that had been her constant companion for six long years, the question that Sarah's absence had allowed her to push to the back of her mind:

If Sarah had not chosen an *Englisch* life, would Daniel have asked Sarah to marry him?

And the even more painful question that inevitably followed:

Have I always been Daniel's second choice?

Miriam swayed, reaching out for one of the farm stand display tables for support. *Stop this!* she told herself fiercely. *Stop this train of thought right now. No good will come of it.*

But Miriam could not stop. She never had been able to stop. That was just the trouble.

In the dark, Miriam began to move around the farm stand, finding her way by touch. She made one circuit of the space, and then another, while her thoughts circled inside her mind.

There were days when it seemed to Miriam that she had lived with the fear of being second best forever, that it went hand in hand and step-by-step with her love for Daniel, getting up with her each morning, going to bed with her each night, until the love and fear were so entwined that they, too, were married and could never be pulled apart. Days when it seemed to her that the greatest task that God had ever charged her with was finding the way to understand, to be at peace with, the confused workings of her own heart.

Miriam stopped walking and then reversed direction. Once again as if following her body's lead, a series of images began to unfurl inside her mind. Daniel, not as the strapping man he now was, but as he had been the day

Miriam first saw him, a wobbly but energetic not-quite-two-year-old. Miriam herself had been all of three at the time. The pair had been in the front yard of Daniel's adoptive parents, the Brennemanns.

Daniel had taken his first steps straight toward Miriam, ending his sudden burst of locomotion with a grab to hold on to her and keep himself upright. The tactic backfired, and they had both tumbled to the ground. But rather than crying, Daniel had simply gazed into Miriam's face with wide, astonished eyes. Miriam gazed right back. For several seconds, neither made a sound. Then Daniel began to laugh, and Miriam had heard her own laughter ring out even as she felt a fierce and sudden love blossom inside her young heart.

Her facility for spontaneous laughter had faded as she had grown, but her love for Daniel had not. Through all the years that followed, she had never lost it. It had remained inside her heart. Years that had seen Miriam grow into a young woman, slim yet strong, and Daniel into a determined, hardworking farmer, reserved and spare in his habits, but who had never quite lost that twinkle, dancing at the very back of his eyes. He was more sure-footed now. The years had certainly changed that. And they had changed something else. They'd changed the direction of Daniel's footsteps, or so it had always seemed to Miriam, so that they no longer led straight to her, but to her younger sister, Sarah.

Sarah, Miriam thought. *Everything always came back to Sarah.* She stopped walking.

Sarah, who was almost exactly Daniel's age, rather than

slightly older, as Miriam was. Sarah, whose quick laughter seemed to be the perfect match for the twinkle that never quite left Daniel's eyes. Miriam had seen these things, even as her heart bled a little at the sight. And she was not so blind that she could not see that pretty much everyone in the district expected that Daniel and Sarah would one day make a match of it. They seemed so well suited, so comfortable when they were together.

And Miriam couldn't help but think that maybe if Daniel had married Sarah, she would have given Daniel children.

Children, Miriam thought. She pressed a hand against her mouth, suppressing a cry, thinking of the months and years that she had been childless. And wondering, as she did every day, if God meant her to be barren. If that were truly His will, then Daniel had chosen the wrong sister.

But Daniel had not married Sarah. That was not the way things had worked out.

Daniel had been baptized almost immediately after his *rumspringa*, just like Miriam. Like her, Daniel had chosen the Plain life. But the months went by and still Sarah made no move to come forward and be baptized. Until finally the day came when she asked to speak to her father and sister together and told them the truth: She was choosing an *Englisch* life. Much as she loved her family, and cherished the way she had been brought up, Sarah believed that the world outside was where her steps were being guided. That was where she truly belonged.

And there was more. Unbeknownst to either Miriam or Jacob, Sarah had continued her education, studying in secret, and had applied and been accepted at a college in far-away San Francisco. She would not simply be leaving the community where she'd grown up, she would be moving three thousand miles away, all the way across the country. There, she would study to become a social worker. It was to this work, she told her father and sister, that she believed she was being called.

"You are sure?" Jacob had asked, after a moment's stunned silence.

By way of answer, Sarah had knelt at her father's feet, placed her hands on his knees, and gazed directly into his eyes.

"As sure as I have been of anything in my life, Daed," she replied.

Miriam's *daed* expelled a great breath, so great a breath that Miriam had been certain there was not an ounce of breath left in her father's body. And then he spoke once more.

"I will miss you, my daughter, but I will also wish you well. For I think you could not make a choice such as this if your heart and feet were not being guided by God. May He give you wings to fly."

Sarah had put her head on her father's knee and wept. Miriam had left the two of them alone. She was stunned that Sarah could make such a request. And she was surprised that Daed had accepted Sarah's choice so easily. Miriam knew that others in the district would judge Daed harshly for giving Sarah his blessing to leave, for raising a daughter who did not join the church. But mostly, she was shocked and hurt that her sister had not confided in her.

How could Sarah keep such a secret from her own sister? Did Sarah mistrust Miriam that much? What other secrets had Sarah kept from her?

That day, like today, Miriam had gone outdoors. She'd wandered aimlessly through the fields for what had felt like hours, trying to sort out her own tumultuous emotions. Only when the sun began to set did she turn her feet toward home.

And it was on the journey back that she had seen Sarah and Daniel together. Sarah speaking earnestly, her face up-turned toward Daniel's bent head. With one hand, she gripped Daniel by the arm. Even from far away, Miriam had felt like a spy, an intruder. But she could not seem to turn away or avert her eyes.

And so she had seen Daniel shake his head. Seen Sarah grip him by the shoulders. And then, as Miriam still watched, Sarah had reached up and Daniel had reached down until the two were in each other's arms. Miriam could see the urgency of the embrace, even from far off. Then Daniel released Sarah, spun on one heel, and walked away. He did not look back, and in the weeks between Sarah's announcement and her departure, Daniel did not visit the Lapp farm. Not even once.

A month to the day after Miriam and Jacob watched Sarah's plane lift off for San Francisco, Daniel asked Miriam to be his wife.

They had been married that winter. Sarah had not come to the wedding. She wrote to say the date fell right in the middle of something called finals week, a series of tests that would prove she had mastered what she had been taught. If she came home then, all her hard work at school would be lost.

I am sorry not to be with you on your wedding day, Sarah had written. *But I wish you happiness with all my heart.*

The six years since then had been both the happiest and the most troubled of Miriam's life. Every day, she awoke to the gift of being Daniel's wife, so full of love for him that it sometimes seemed impossible her heart could contain it all. But every night when she lay down beside him and closed her eyes, the image of that long-ago embrace flickered for a fraction of an instant inside Miriam's eyelids. Nothing she did could ever banish it entirely. And as the years passed and still she and Daniel had no children, that image of her husband and sister together, the image of what might have been, had slowly eaten a hole into Miriam's heart until fear and love resided there side by side.

Was Daniel sorry he had chosen her instead of Sarah? Did he still love Sarah, even after all this time?

"Miriam?" a quiet voice behind her said.

Miriam spun around. A figure was outlined against the block of light that was the open back door. *How bright it is outside!* Miriam thought. Full day. She had been in the farm stand much longer than she realized.

"I thought that I might find you here," Daniel said. He did not come into the farm stand, but stayed right where he was. "Are you well? Do you want me to turn on the light?"

"No," Miriam said at once, answering the second question first. "And I am fine. I just—"

"I understand," Daniel said. "This place will always be your father's, won't it?"

11

"Ja," Miriam said, as her heart flooded with love for this good man who was her husband. Even in the dark, he saw so much. So why was it that he could not see the one thing Miriam hoped for the most? How very much she needed to know he loved her, that she was first in his heart.

"Are you ready to go up to the house?" Daniel asked. "The others will begin arriving soon. Bishop John and his wife are already there. Leah, their niece, baked you the coffee cake you liked so much at the last worship Sunday."

"That is kind of her."

She moved toward the open door. Daniel stepped outside and Miriam followed, blinking against the sudden light. While Daniel waited patiently, Miriam closed and locked the farm stand door. As she turned toward him, Daniel extended one hand, the faintest question in his blue eyes. Miriam hesitated just a moment, and then linked her fingers with her husband's. Daniel's grip was sure and strong. Miriam's love for him rose like a great flood inside her heart.

Please, God, she thought. *If it is Your will, let Daniel and I walk heart in heart as we now walk side by side.*

And what if that isn't His will? a voice inside her asked.

"Are you ready?" Daniel asked softly.

"I am ready," Miriam said, temporarily banishing the voice of doubt.

Together they walked up the hill toward the farmhouse in the bright morning sunshine.

Two

Miriam twisted her hands in her lap, battling the urge to turn her body around on the hard wooden bench so that she could see the entrance to the barn. All morning, people had been arriving for the funeral service. Amos Shetler had come first, driving his wagon with the long bed that would carry Jacob's coffin to the *graabhof*, where her father would be buried. Amos's oldest sons, Samuel and Ben, had taken charge of buggy parking, while the youngest, Enos, had stayed near the farm stand, showing *Englischers* where to park their cars. In next to no time, or so it seemed to Miriam, the big Lapp barn had filled almost to bursting with all those who had come to honor her father.

But Sarah had not yet arrived.

Where can she be? Miriam wondered. She stopped twisting her fingers to pluck nervously at her dark apron. Without warning, she felt strong yet gentle fingers close over hers. She started, and then turned to face Rachel Miller, Bishop John Miller's wife, who was seated at her right side. The spot on Miriam's left side was empty, waiting for Sarah. As she met Rachel's calm, dark eyes, Miriam felt the prick of tears at the back of her own.

"Dear Miriam," Rachel said in a low voice. "I'm sure Sarah will be here soon. Perhaps you should wait by the door. I'm sure your sister will appreciate seeing you the moment she arrives. She has made a long, sad journey to come here."

Miriam shook her head, as if to dispel the thoughts that so troubled her. "How did you know what I was thinking?"

Rachel gave Miriam's hands a last squeeze and then let go. "It's only common sense," she said. "This is an important day for you and for Sarah. Go wait for her. It will make you feel better. And do not worry. No one is going to start the service without both of Jacob's girls."

Grateful for Rachel's understanding, Miriam rose and turned toward the entrance to the barn. Bright sunlight streamed in through the open double doors. As was the tradition in worship services, the men and boys sat on one side of the barn, and the women and girls sat facing them on the other. Miriam gazed out across a sea of dark dresses and aprons, the fronts of the women's white *kapps* peeking out from the black head coverings they wore for the funeral. Across the center aisle, the shoulders of the men in their sober black frock coats they donned only for serious occasions brushed together. Miriam saw the scattering of dark *Englisch* dress among the crowd.

Out of the corner of her eye, Miriam saw Daniel start to rise to his feet as well. And then, suddenly, all of Miriam's attention was claimed by the shape of a woman carving a dark outline into the bright square of the open doors. Could this be Sarah at last? Quickly, Miriam hurried down the aisle. The figure in the doorway took a few tentative steps, as if uncertain where to go, or perhaps it was just that her eyes were having trouble adjusting to the softer light of the barn after the brightness of the outdoors.

As she approached, Miriam could see that the woman was wearing a simple black dress with a row of dark buttons down the front of the bodice. A triangle of dark lace covered her pale blond hair, which was cut in a chin-length bob. She wore sheer black stockings and a pair of high-heeled black shoes. In spite of herself, Miriam felt her footsteps falter. Could this, this stylish *Englisch* woman, really be Sarah?

She looks like a stranger, she thought. The last time Sarah had visited, she had come in Plain clothes. Miriam remembered her saying that she'd put them on before leaving for the airport, so she would fit back in easily. And now, did she no longer want to fit in, to be part of them?

Sarah started forward, her hands outstretched. "Miriam," she breathed. Her hands found Miriam's and held on tight. "Oh, Miriam, I'm so sorry. The taxi had a flat tire, and it took forever to get it sorted out. I was so afraid I wouldn't make it in time. I hope you didn't worry."

"You are here now," Miriam answered as she returned her sister's tight grip. "It's all right. Everything will be all right."

And, suddenly, just like that, it was.

The grip of Sarah's fingers felt just as they always had, strong but also trusting, as firmly connected to her as when they were children. It didn't matter what she looked like or how long she had been gone. It didn't matter that she had chosen an *Englisch* life, and Miriam, a Plain one. It didn't even matter that Miriam was now a married woman, that her last name was Brennemann now. With their hands clasped tightly together, they were the Lapp girls, here to honor the father they both loved.

"I saved you a place right beside me," Miriam said.

Right where you belong.

Hands still tightly clasped, the sisters walked together to take their place at this last tribute to their father.

Several hours later, under a hot noonday sun, Miriam stood in the graveyard, gazing down at her father's grave. A gentle mound of earth now covered Jacob Lapp's final resting place, but Miriam knew that the earth would settle in the days to come. Wind, rain, and sun would do their work, and soon the grass would begin to grow. The place where her father lay would no longer look fresh and new, like a sudden interruption. It would look like it belonged.

In the days since her father's death, Miriam had tried to imagine this moment. What would she feel as she gazed at the graves of her parents, now resting side by side? What final wish or image of her father would flit, quick as a hummingbird, across her mind? But now that the moment had actually arrived, it was as if Miriam had no conscious thought at all. Instead, a clear, bright light seemed to flood her entire being. In it, there was no place for words, and no need for them. Miriam was filled, as she was absolutely certain Jacob was, with the light of the grace of God.

"Miriam?" she heard a voice say softly. Automatically, she turned toward the sound and found herself looking up into Daniel's face. Only then did Miriam realize that tears were streaming down her cheeks. She could see them, see herself, reflected in her husband's eyes.

Ach, Daniel's eyes . . . they are beautiful, so beautiful! Miriam thought. Even here, in these circumstances, the color of Daniel's eyes had the power to take Miriam's breath away, to take her by surprise. They were a blue so vivid they had always inspired one of Miriam's rare flights of fancy, for it had always seemed to her that Daniel's eyes must be made from a slice of summer sky.

As she looked into them now, Miriam saw both a question and a reassurance. She reached up and touched Daniel's cheek in silent thanks, watched his eyes light with surprise. He reached to cover her hand with one of his own. With his other hand, he offered her a white handkerchief. She took it and wiped the tears from her face.

"I'll go tell Rachel that we will be up at the house soon," Daniel said. "You stay with Sarah. I'll be back in a few—"

"I can't stay with Sarah," Miriam protested. "I don't know where she is. She's gone. She was here a minute ago. But after we finished the Lord's Prayer, I . . ."

She stopped as a strange expression flitted across Daniel's face.

"Miriam," he said softly, "Sarah is standing right behind you."

Miriam swung around. Sure enough, Sarah was right behind her, staring at their father's grave. Her eyes were sad but without tears.

"I'm sorry for disappearing so suddenly like that," she said. Her gaze met Miriam's and then skittered away. "I'm not sure quite what happened, in all honesty. There was just something about all the people and seeing the grave being filled up, shovelful by shovelful. I just . . ." Her voice trailed off.

"I can understand how it might be difficult," Daniel said, his voice soothing. "It's been years since you've been home. And then, to come back to this . . ."

"Thank you for saying that, Daniel," Sarah answered. Was it just Miriam's imagination, or were her sister's cheeks stained with just the faintest blush? "Your words are very kind."

"You are looking well, Sarah," Daniel replied.

Sarah gave a snort of not particularly amused laughter. "I *look* like I sat in a plane all night long. Miriam is the one who looks well, don't you think?" The compliment increased Miriam's discomfort. It was not their way to talk about appearances.

"Daniel!" A voice from a short distance away cut across the awkwardness of the moment.

"Is that Lucas?" Sarah asked.

"*Ja*. You haven't forgotten us after all," Daniel answered

with a smile. He turned toward his younger brother and called, "I'm coming!" He turned back to Miriam and Sarah. "I'll return with the buggy in a few moments. Then we can all go back to the house. I'm sure Mamm and Rachel will have everything ready by the time we return."

Now that the funeral and the rituals of burial were over, most of the mourners would be returning to their own homes. But some, those who were particularly close to Daniel and Miriam or who had traveled a long distance to attend, would return to the Lapp farmhouse for a meal before heading home. Like almost everything else that had happened since Jacob's death, the meal was being prepared by family and friends—in this case, Daniel's mother, Amelia; his sister-in-law, Annaliese; and Rachel, Bishop John's wife.

Daniel made a half gesture, as if to touch Miriam's shoulder, then stopped short. Without another word, he turned on one heel and strode off. Miriam and Sarah were left standing beside their father's grave, alone.

"I don't know how to do it, Miriam," Sarah said. "I thought about it on the plane, all night long. I was hoping, once I was actually standing here, that I could find the way, but I can't seem to. I don't know how to tell Daed good-bye."

A quick pang of sympathy speared through Miriam. She had been given the gift of several days beside her father's body, praying and saying good-bye. But Sarah had not received this gift. She no longer lived at home, no longer lived a Plain life.

Miriam reached to put an arm around her sister's shoulders. "Maybe you don't have to," she suggested. "Not today, anyhow. Let it go for now, Sarah. Try to be at peace with God."

"I *am* trying," Sarah said, and Miriam heard the catch in her sister's voice. "But I've never been as good at that as you are, you know."

"I always think of you as being good at everything," Miriam said, surprised.

Sarah shook her head. "No," she said, "you're the one who's always been such a quick study." She smiled at Miriam. "Even in San Francisco, I've never met anyone who's so capable."

Miriam didn't know how to answer that; it was so different from her perception. It always seemed to her that things came easily to her sister. Sarah was the one who seemed so good at everything—at sewing and baking and quilting and putting up preserves. She had a talent for singing and gardening. She even had a knack for working with the animals. Miriam remembered an ornery rooster who used to follow her sister everywhere. Sarah was the only one who could get near him without being pecked half to death.

Miriam felt the breeze come up. It lifted the strings of her *kapp* and set them to fluttering. Miriam followed their dance with her eyes. Her eyes fell on the plain stone marking her mother's grave. There would be one for her father before the month was out. Her parents, so long separated by the early death of her mother, were together at last, safe in the arms of a merciful and loving God. She gave Sarah's shoulders a squeeze and then let go.

"Sarah, do you remember Mamm?" she asked.

"Not really." Sarah shook her head. "Do you?"

"A little bit, least I think so," Miriam answered, as the image she remembered most clearly sprang into her mind.

The figure of a woman leaning over her bed, tucking in the covers with sure and gentle fingers before bending low to give Miriam a kiss good night. Their breath made soft white clouds in the night air. It was winter, and the upstairs bedrooms were cold. The light of the kerosene lamp filled the room with its pale glow. But try as she might, Miriam had never been able to bring her mother's features into focus. Edna Lapp's face remained a blank, her form little more than a smooth, dark outline.

"Did you ever wonder why Daed never married again?" Miriam asked.

"Of course I did." Sarah nodded. "I used to wonder all the time. And then I'd try to picture what life would be like if he chose this woman or that one."

"You didn't!" Miriam exclaimed. She turned her head to stare at Sarah.

Sarah's jaw was set and her face slightly flushed. "Oh, yes, I did," she replied, her tone making it all too clear that these memories were not particularly happy ones. "Remember all those stomachaches I used to get right at bedtime? It's because I was imagining how different things would be once Daed married again."

"You never told me."

Sarah's expression softened. "I know. I think it's because I knew what you'd say, even when we were small. 'There's no point letting your imagination get away from you, Sarah. Whatever comes, it will be God's will.'"

"I did not sound like that," Miriam protested.

At this, Sarah actually smiled. "You did so. But in all fairness, I don't think it was your fault. You must have heard one of the grown-ups say something like it about a thousand times. And if you *had* said it, you would have been right. Not that I would have admitted it at the time, of course." Sarah studied Miriam with curiosity. "Did *you* want Daed to get married again?"

Miriam shook her head. "No. To tell you the truth, I was always relieved that he did not. I liked things with just the three of us. Though lately I've sometimes wished . . ."

Startled, Miriam broke off. Had she really been about to confess that it was only since her marriage to Daniel that she had wished for a mother? Someone she could turn to with all those questions new brides always had. And yes, someone to whom she could pour out her heart. To share the pain of being childless. That pain and the fear of always being second best were things Miriam knew she must keep to herself.

How did you feel, Mamm? she thought now. *Did you have someone to talk to, to confide in?*

Jacob and Edna had been married for more than ten years before Miriam came along. How had her mother coped with all those years of being childless? How had she handled the fear that they might go on forever? Had she, like Miriam, sometimes thought that a life without children just might break her heart?

"Here comes Daniel," Sarah said. She placed a hand on Miriam's arm. Even through the fabric of her dress, Miriam could feel how cold her sister's fingers were. She pulled Sarah's hand into the crook of her arm, covering her sister's fingers with her own to warm them. Sarah made a soft sound and pressed her other hand to her mouth.

"Rachel says she and my mother are taking care of everything up at the house," Daniel said as he approached. "She tells you to take your time."

"There's not enough time in the world," Sarah said, her voice suddenly bitter. She gave her whole body a shake, as if literally trying to throw off her sorrow.

"Are you all right?" Miriam asked her.

Sarah nodded. "I'm sorry I spoke so sharply."

"You don't have to apologize. I understand," Miriam told her. "Losing Daed is not easy for any of us."

Sarah drew in a deep breath, as if steeling herself for whatever was to come next. "I am ready whenever the two of you are. I think that I would like to go back to the house—I mean, back home."

Home, Miriam thought, where everything would look the same but be so different. It had not been Sarah's home for the last six years. And now it was no longer Daed's home. Miriam wasn't sure it even felt like her home anymore. How would they all pick themselves up and go on?

What had she just counseled Sarah? *Let it go, for now.* Because for now that was all she could do. Perhaps, day by day, if they all trusted in God, the house would begin to feel like home again, the place that Miriam loved best of all.

Her arm still linked through Sarah's, Miriam took the arm that Daniel offered, so that all three of them were joined. Then she turned away from her father's grave.

"Yes," she said. "Let us all go home."

Three

The next morning, Miriam was up early. *When am I not?* she thought with a smile. But today's up early was different. Today, she would return to the daily tasks she found so meaningful, the ones that, added together, day by day, made up her life.

She had already started cooking breakfast. The scent of coffee filled the air. Bacon sizzled in a cast-iron skillet on top of the stove. Miriam retrieved several eggs from the propane refrigerator. With quick, practiced motions, she broke them into a bowl, setting the eggshells aside. Later, she would use the shells to compost the garden. They were good for the roses, and Miriam's rose hip jelly was one of the farm stand's best sellers.

Miriam stirred the eggs with a fork, adding salt, pepper,

and a little water. She turned the bacon in the pan, and then brought out the pie that her mother-in-law, Amelia, had left for them. It was the first time since Miriam and Daniel had been married that Miriam was serving her husband a pie she had not made herself. But she had been very touched by Amelia's gesture. Clearly, she knew her oldest son well.

The bacon done to her liking, Miriam lifted it from the pan and set it on a plate lined with a paper towel. She blotted any extra grease, and then set the plate in the oven where the pilot light would help keep it warm. She drained some of the grease off from the cast-iron pan, glancing out the window as she did so. She didn't want to start the eggs until she knew Daniel was coming in. That way, they would be nice and hot.

As Miriam watched, Daniel came out of the barn and started across the yard. He moved with purpose, as he invariably did. It had always seemed to Miriam that Daniel knew precisely where he was going. It was one of the things that she loved best about him. Not that she could predict where he would end up! Though she was pretty sure she knew his destination at the moment. As Miriam continued to watch, Daniel paused at the pump partway between the house and the barn.

He almost always did this when the weather was fine, a holdover from his boyhood when Amelia required that the boys wash up before they came indoors. Daniel was a grown man now, with a house of his own. He no longer had to wash his hands and face in the yard. But, as long as the weather was warm enough, he typically did it anyhow.

It always made Miriam shake her head, half in exasperation, half in love.

As Miriam continued to watch, Daniel worked the pump handle vigorously. After a few moments, water gushed from the spout. Daniel stopped pumping and thrust first his hands, and then his face, into the flow before it stopped. He stepped backward quickly and tossed back his head, sending water drops flying. Though she'd seen him perform this ritual almost every summer's day for six years now, the fact that Daniel could get his face wet yet still keep the front of his shirt dry never lost the ability to take Miriam by surprise. She had teased him about it, not long after they were married.

Practice makes perfect. Daniel had quoted the *Englisch* saying with a smile.

With one last shake of his blond head, Daniel continued on toward the house. Miriam stepped away from the window and walked briskly across the kitchen to meet her husband at the kitchen door. Without a word, she handed him a clean towel. Daniel took it from her, just as silent, but Miriam was pretty sure she caught a glimpse of Daniel's eyes, dancing with laughter, just before he buried his face in the towel.

"All clean?" she inquired as he lifted his head.

"What do you think?" Daniel asked. He tilted his face for inspection. Miriam regarded it seriously.

"Let's see the hands as well."

Daniel held them out, palms up, then, after a moment, he turned them palms down.

"I believe you will do," Miriam declared.

"Thank you," Daniel answered formally. Then he smiled. He took a deep breath. "Is that bacon I smell?"

"It is indeed," Miriam said. "Now that you are clean enough for them, I'll start the eggs. Sit down." She moved to the stove as Daniel poured himself a cup of coffee, and then took his place at the table. "Your mother left a pie."

"Did she?" Daniel said. "That was kind of her. I'll remember to thank her when I see her later today." There was a brief silence. "What kind?"

Miriam tested the skillet before tipping in the eggs. She was glad her back was turned so that Daniel couldn't see her smile. "Rhubarb. The last from her garden, she said."

"Ach," Daniel said. "Well, that is nice."

It was his favorite kind.

Miriam fell silent, stirring the scrambled eggs. They didn't take long. She turned off the burner, and then used a clean dish towel to pull the plate of bacon from the oven, together with the clean plates that rested just beneath it. Miriam scooped a healthy portion of eggs onto Daniel's plate, added several rashers of bacon, and, finally, a good-sized piece of the rhubarb pie. If she knew her husband, he'd have a second piece before he headed out to the fields. She turned from the counter, crossed the short distance to the table, and set the plate in front of him.

"Danki," Daniel said.

"You're welcome," Miriam replied. She turned back to the counter to prepare her own plate. "Oh," she exclaimed softly.

"What?" Daniel asked quickly. He started to get up. "Are you all right? Did you burn yourself?"

"No, it's nothing like that," Miriam said. "It's just . . ." She took a steadying breath. "I got out three plates, just like always, only I didn't even realize I'd done it until now."

"But surely the third plate is for Sarah," Daniel said.

"*Ja*, it can be for Sarah," Miriam replied. *But that isn't why I got it out,* she thought. *That isn't it at all.* Instead, she had warmed three plates just the way she always did, one for Daniel, one for her, and one for her father. "I'll just keep it warm," she said, not wanting to have to explain.

"Sarah sleeps late now," he observed. "Do you think she's taking on the *Englisch* ways?"

"She was on a plane the whole night before the funeral," Miriam reminded him, surprised to find herself defending her sister. "It's good that she's catching up on her sleep."

Using the dish towel once again, Miriam returned the plate to the oven. She dished up her own breakfast, poured herself a cup of coffee, and sat down opposite her husband. Daniel bowed his head for the silent blessing, and Miriam did, too. They gave thanks for the food and the day to come.

Daniel ate the same way he did most things, Miriam thought as she watched him pick up his fork and tackle the eggs, economically, with no wasted motions. It wasn't that he rushed. She didn't think she had ever really seen Daniel hurry, unless the occasion truly called for it. He simply applied himself, with *dedication*. She smiled to herself as Daniel plunged his fork into the pie and scooped up a big bite. Miriam followed suit, though her bite was smaller.

The pie *was* good. Miriam had a deft hand with pie herself, but Amelia had a special touch. No two ways about it.

"You are going to help Lucas to bring in his wheat today?" she asked.

On any given day, Miriam knew what Daniel's tasks would be as well as she knew her own. There was a rhythm, a progression to farm life. The fact that neither she nor Daniel had performed their usual duties during their period of mourning did not make that rhythm go away.

"Yes." Daniel nodded. He took a sip of coffee to wash down the pie. "Then Lucas and the boys will come to us." Daniel was one of five brothers. There were two girls in the Brennemann family as well. Martin and Amelia Brennemann had adopted Daniel when he was just an infant, after his parents were killed in a buggy accident. Daniel and Lucas, the Brennemanns' next-oldest son, were a little less than a year apart in age.

"Lucas and I have been speaking of going to the horse auction next month," Daniel continued. "I've been thinking of getting another field horse." He smiled at her. "I will miss your *daed*'s company there. He had a fine eye for horses. If it wasn't for Jacob, I would never have even noticed Major."

Major was Daniel's favorite draft horse, a calm, powerful Percheron who, when they first saw him at the auction, had been a scrawny, frightened colt. Only her father had seen the horse's potential.

"Yes, you and Lucas should go," Miriam replied, feeling a tug of grief. Her father had loved going to the big auctions. Men came from districts all around, and it was a good time to reconnect with old friends and acquaintances. This would be the first time in decades that Jacob Lapp would not be there, studying the horses and freely giving his advice to his friends.

"You will go to the farm stand this morning?" Daniel asked.

"*Ja.*" Miriam nodded. She took a sip of coffee as she considered. "I won't open for business until tomorrow, but I want to tidy up and take stock." She sent Daniel a quick smile. "Today, I will even turn the lights on."

"I am pleased to hear it. It is the one building where we pay for electricity, and yet I found my wife standing there in the dark," he teased her gently.

"Not today," she promised.

Daniel pulled in a breath as if to say something else, then changed his mind. Instead, he took another bite of pie.

"You will want some help there, I think," he finally said when he had finished chewing.

Miriam nodded. The whole time Daed was dying, she had known she would have to come up with a new plan for running the farm stand. It now belonged to her and Daniel, as did the farm itself. But Daniel had never taken an active part in the day-to-day running of the stand. This was only as it should be. He had the farm itself to run.

It was Jacob who had kept the farm stand going, particularly after the *Englisch* doctors had told him that his heart was weak, that the exertion of working in the fields could be dangerous for his health. But being idle was not the Plain way, so Jacob had devoted himself to the farm stand instead. Though he had started it when the girls were young, after his diagnosis he poured all of his attention into it, and the whole community felt the benefit of his efforts, with the proceeds providing much-needed additional income—income that would be lost if the stand were closed. Virtually every family in the district now sold something at the stand.

To Miriam's amazement, the stand had developed a reputation among the *Englischers*. Locals and tourists who stayed in the area all stopped at the stand. Miriam had sold Plain goods to people from New York, New Jersey, Ohio, West Virginia, even California. The farm stand was better, they said, than any city farmers' market. Miriam knew she not only had to keep the stand going, but she had to maintain the high quality of the produce and products that Jacob had offered.

"I'll need help," Miriam agreed. She glanced toward the head of the table, where her father had always sat. It was rightfully Daniel's spot now, and she knew he had not yet taken it out of respect for her grief. "But figuring out how it is best to manage will take some time. I am hoping that Sarah will help while she is here, but . . ." Miriam let her voice trail off.

"But Sarah will not stay." Daniel finished her thought.

Miriam shook her head. "No, Sarah will not stay. She'll go back to San Francisco at the end of the summer. I need someone *here*, especially through the fall harvest."

"Perhaps we should speak to Bishop John," Daniel suggested. "He might know of someone."

"That's a good thought," Miriam acknowledged, even as she felt tears rise in her eyes. It would never again be her and Daed working side by side in the stand, so used to each other's ways that they worked seamlessly, each knowing exactly what was needed. She would have to get used to working with someone new. Distressed, she pushed back from the table, snatched up her plate, and moved quickly to the sink.

"Miriam." Behind her, she heard the scrape of Daniel's chair as he, too, rose. A moment later, she felt his strong hands on her shoulders. Miriam wavered just for a moment. Then she turned into her husband's arms.

Here, right here, she thought. This was where she longed to be; this was where she belonged. Daniel was so strong and solid, like a great tree that no storm could ever bring down. She felt so sheltered and protected within the circle of his embrace.

Please, she thought. *Let the world stop, just for a few moments.* These few moments when she was in her husband's arms.

"I am sorry," Daniel said quietly. "I did not mean to upset you. Your father was a good man. I miss him, too, and I know that it is hard to lose him, even though we both know that he is with God. But at least Sarah is home, if only for a little while. You can get to know each other again, and she can be some help for you."

Instantly, Miriam stiffened. Must he always speak of Sarah?

As if he sensed some change in her, Daniel moved back a little, though he kept his arms around her. However small it was, she felt this new distance between them keenly.

"Yes," she said, managing to keep her voice smooth and

even, though she could not bring herself to look up into Daniel's eyes. "It will be good to have her help."

And she stepped out of her husband's arms.

A half hour later, Miriam stood in front of the farm stand, surveying her handiwork. The big front double doors of the stand were thrown open wide. Above the opening, directly in the center, the carved wooden sign that proclaimed "Stony Field Farm Stand" looked welcoming and cheerful in the bright sunshine.

By dint of much huffing and puffing, Miriam had managed to tug the first of the display tables out into position in front of the open doors. It had been something of a challenge. The tables were sturdy and heavy. Moving them in and out was usually a two-person job. Truly, she hadn't needed to do it. After all, she wouldn't be opening for business until the following day. But this was the first day that she felt the stand belonged to her, and she needed to prove to herself that she was perfectly able to set up and run it on her own if need be, that her *daed*'s faith in her hadn't been misplaced. What had Sarah called her? Capable. She had to be worthy of Sarah's faith, too.

I really should have waited for Sarah, she thought. But Miriam didn't want to wait. She wanted to get going *now.* The farm stand was her responsibility, her challenge, one she was determined to meet. She marched back inside the stand, seized the second table, gave it a quick tug to get it moving, then continued to drag it carefully toward the open doors. Too fast, and she was afraid that she might scratch the wooden floor.

Miriam felt the threshold bump against her heels. She stepped over it carefully, pulling the front legs of the table out into the yard. *Just a little farther now.* She pulled a little harder. The table shot forward, the back legs catching on the threshold. The front edge of the table slipped from Miriam's fingers. One of the front legs came down on her foot so hard she saw stars. With a sharp cry, she yanked her foot back, hopping up and down.

"Miriam! *Miriam!*" cried a high, clear voice behind her. "Are you all right?"

Miriam stopped hopping, trying not to wince as she put her full weight on her foot and turned to face the newcomer. Standing behind her was a young woman of about sixteen. She had blond hair and blue eyes, just as Miriam did. At the moment, her eyes were wide with concern. She was breathing quickly, as if she had just run a race.

It was Leah Gingerich, Rachel Miller's niece. She lived with Rachel and Bishop John. "*Gude mariye*, Leah," Miriam said.

"*Gude mariye,*" Leah answered, giving the polite response. But she went on almost at once, as if she simply could not contain herself. "Oh, Miriam!" she burst out. "Are you sure that you're all right? That looked like it hurt so much!"

"It did," Miriam admitted, feeling her lips tug upward into a smile. Leah's energy was infectious. "Though to tell you the truth, not so much that I didn't have time to think about how silly I must have looked, hopping up and down."

"But you didn't!" Leah exclaimed. "Well," she amended, "at least not much. But I'm pretty sure I would have cried like a *boppli* if that had happened to me."

"My eyes had no room for tears," Miriam said, her smile growing larger. "They were too busy seeing stars!"

"Ouch," Leah said sympathetically.

"Ja," Miriam said. "Ouch. But what can I do for you, Leah? The farm stand isn't open yet."

"I know." Leah nodded at once. "But I thought perhaps you might be here. You and Jacob always opened the farm stand first thing in the morning, and I . . ."

Her voice trailed off. *It's the first time I've ever seen her at a loss for words,* Miriam thought. It wasn't that Leah chattered. But she did seem to have the habit of saving up her words and then sending them all out together in one great big rush. This, together with Leah's petite frame, made her seem younger than she actually was. But Miriam was almost certain she remembered that Leah had recently announced her desire to be baptized. That would make her sixteen at least. Old enough for courting.

"I want to help."

Leah's voice jerked Miriam back to the present.

"What?"

"I want to help," Leah said once more. "I want to learn everything I can about how to run a farm stand so that, maybe someday, I can have one of my own. You will need help now, won't you, now that your father is gone? I'll do any job you like. I'm a hard worker, you can ask my *aenti* Rachel. She'll tell you."

"Whoa," Miriam said, holding up her hands. "Slow down. Give me a moment to think, Leah."

Leah swallowed hard. For several humming moments, neither woman spoke. Leah's hands were clasped tightly in front of her, her eyes fixed on the ground. Gazing at her unexpected visitor, trying to assemble her scattered thoughts, Miriam realized suddenly that Leah was wearing a pair of plastic clogs the exact same shade of green as her own. For no reason she could account for, this tipped the scales.

"Tell me something, Leah," she said. "How do you feel about dusting?"

Leah's gaze shot to Miriam's face. In her blue eyes, Miriam saw surprise. And also, she thought, just the faintest hint of dismay.

"I will be happy to dust, if that will help, Miriam," Leah answered solemnly.

Miriam smiled. *Surely the hand of God is in this,* she thought. Hadn't she been considering going to see Bishop John to discuss the farm stand just this morning? And now here was the bishop's niece, offering to help.

"I will tell you a secret, Leah," she said. "I have never cared for dusting, myself. It is tedious work, but it goes much better when there are extra hands to help. What do you say we work together for a while? After that, if you still want to help, we can walk to your *aenti* and *onkel*'s house and I will speak with Rachel."

"Oh, *thank you*, Miriam!" Leah said, her eyes shining. "What shall we dust first? Where do you keep the dust cloths?"

Miriam got the cleaning supplies from the broom closet her *daed* had built. She set Leah to her first task, dusting the shelves of jams and preserves. Leah went to work with such a serious, determined expression that Miriam realized she had hardly stopped smiling since Leah arrived. Oh, yes, Miriam thought, Leah might be exactly what she needed.

Four

"I just don't understand it," Leah said. She stepped out the front doors of the farm stand and gave her rag a brisk snap that sent the dust flying. Her tone was filled with such exasperation and outrage that Miriam bit back a smile.

The two had worked steadily all morning, dusting and sweeping and generally putting the farm stand to rights. Miriam had kept one ear cocked for Sarah, thinking her sister might come down to the farm stand once she was up. But so far, she had not arrived. Now it was almost time for the midday meal.

"The farm stand has only been closed for just over a week," Leah went on as she came back inside. "How can things have gotten so dusty in so short a time?"

"Dust is a mystery," Miriam admitted. "I think that's

why it's such a trial." She gave her own rag a snap, then returned it to the basket where it was kept. Later she would take the rags they had used today up to the farmhouse to be washed.

"But I think that is enough dusting for one day," she went on. "Come, put your rag in the basket and let's get the tables back inside. Then we can go and see Rachel."

Leah added her rag to the basket and followed Miriam outside. Miriam took the near end of the table, and Leah the far end. That meant that Miriam would be the one walking backward.

"Watch your feet," Miriam said as they maneuvered the first of the big display tables back inside the farm stand and prepared to set it down.

Leah smiled. "These tables will not get the better of me," she said. "I have my eye on them."

Once both the tables were back inside the stand, Miriam swung the big double doors closed and slid home the bolt that locked them. Then Miriam switched off the overhead lights. She and Leah let themselves out the back door, and Miriam locked up behind them. Even after all these years, it still felt strange to lock the doors, she thought. The doors to the farmhouse were never locked. But the house stood well back from the road and was partly hidden from view by a gentle swell of the rolling hills that were so much a part of the landscape of the area. The farm stand was in plain view, right off the road.

Daed didn't like locking up, either, she thought. But her father was sensible in this, as in so much else, and locking up was the sensible choice.

Miriam and Leah crossed to the far side of the road and then walked along the pavement, facing in the direction of whatever traffic might come along, as they made their way to the Millers' farm. Leah had come to live with her *aenti* and *onkel* when she was still a small child. She had originally come only to visit while her parents took a trip to see distant relatives in another part of the country. The driver of the motor coach they were traveling in fell asleep at the wheel, and the coach had gone off the road. It had plunged into a river, and everyone on board had been killed. Leah had lived with Rachel and John Miller ever since.

"What do you think we will have to sell tomorrow?" Leah asked as she and Miriam walked along. "I will check with Aenti Rachel, but I think we still have some late-season raspberries we can sell, and the blackberries are coming on."

"We have raspberries, too, and so will Amelia Brennemann and several others." Miriam nodded. "That will be good for the stand. Berries are always popular with the *Englischers*, and the weekend is coming up."

"How do you know what to sell?" Leah asked. "How do people know what to bring you? Do they just come to the stand with whatever they have? What if they bring something that you don't want?"

"Slow down, Leah!" Miriam said with a smile. "One thing at a time. You will understand how things work once you get started. Besides, I like best to learn things by doing them, don't you?"

"I do," Leah said, her voice surprised. "How did you know? But I like to plan things, too," she added, before Miriam could respond.

"Some planning ahead is good," Miriam agreed. "But we cannot plan too much. The workings of the world are in God's hands, not ours."

"Of course." Leah nodded. They walked in silence for several moments.

While Miriam and Leah had been setting the farm stand to rights, the day had grown warm. The sun was a great ball of orange in the blue, blue sky. *The color of Daniel's eyes,* Miriam thought. At the thought of Daniel, a familiar ache settled in the center of Miriam's chest. *No, not today,* she thought. Not on this morning that had turned out so fine. A breeze had sprung up, ruffling the grass at the side of the road. Miriam took a deep breath, savoring the scents of the world all around her. She would have known the men in the fields were bringing in the wheat just by breathing in. The whole world smelled fresh and green. Beneath her clogs, she could feel the pavement of the road was growing warm.

"Sarah and I used to take turns seeing how far down this road we could walk with our shoes off on a summer day," Miriam mused. "The pavement gets so hot."

"Who won?" Leah asked, her voice intrigued.

"Do you know," Miriam said, "I honestly can't recall. What I remember most is the feel of this road beneath my feet. It seems I have been walking along it my whole life. Probably because I have been!" she added with a quick laugh. "Goodness! I don't know what's gotten into me to be thinking of that all of a sudden."

It was Sarah, she realized. Sarah came home and a world of memories surfaced, so many of them sweet ones.

The two women reached a driveway branching off to the

left and turned down it. Set closer to the road than the Lapp farmhouse, the Millers' house soon came into view.

"Oh, look!" Leah said. "There's Aenti Rachel."

Up ahead, Miriam could see that Rachel Miller had come to stand on the house's wide front porch. Two tall oak trees stood nearby, one at either end of the white clapboard house, spreading cool shade along the grass.

Miriam had always felt a closeness with Rachel. She had a quiet, patient way about her that made it easy to be with her. But she also had a sparkle in her eye that seemed to say "I may be the bishop's wife but I have a little mischief in me, too." Leah waved, and her *aenti* waved back.

"*Wilkomm*, Miriam," Rachel called. She walked down the porch steps and into the yard. "I guessed that Leah had found you when she did not return. I hope she has been helpful."

"*Danki*, Rachel," Miriam replied as she drew near. "And yes, Leah has been very helpful this morning. In fact, I—"

"Oh, Aenti Rachel!" Leah burst out. "Miriam has said that I may work at the farm stand! Isn't it wonderful? If you and my *onkel* give your permission, of course," she added quickly.

"Leah," Rachel said quietly.

Leah's cheeks flamed bright red. She swallowed audibly. But she turned to Miriam at once. "I interrupted you, Miriam," she said. "I am sorry."

"Thank you, Leah," Miriam said, doing her best not to smile. It was hard to feel stern in the face of so much enthusiasm. "I accept your apology." She laid a gentle hand on the girl's arm.

"But Leah is right," Miriam said to Rachel. "In fact, her visit could not have been better timed. Just this morning I was wondering how I would manage at the stand on my own. If you and John give your permission, I'll be glad to have Leah's help."

"Go into the house and set the table for dinner, please, Leah," Rachel said firmly, but her voice was not unkind. Over Leah's head, her eyes met Miriam's. In them, Miriam detected the hint of a smile. "I'll be right along, but I would like to speak to Miriam for a moment."

Miriam gave Leah's arm a quick pat. Casting one beseeching look back over her shoulder, Leah climbed the steps to the porch and went into the house.

"I hope you will forgive her outburst," Rachel said as soon as her niece was indoors. She made a gesture of invitation, and together the two women walked around the side of the house toward the kitchen garden. "Leah is growing into a fine young woman, but I fear she is a little . . . enthusiastic sometimes."

Miriam smiled. "I like her," she said. "And I meant what I said. If you and John are willing, I would be happy to have Leah's help. Over breakfast this morning, Daniel and I were discussing finding some help for the stand."

Miriam paused when they reached the side yard and Rachel's large kitchen garden came into view, with its neatly planted rows of tomatoes, beans, corn, berries, summer squashes, and herbs. "My," she said, "your garden does look fine."

"God has blessed us with particularly good weather this year, I think," Rachel responded. Together the two women began to stroll between the rows. "A good amount of rain when we needed it, and now it is warm but not too hot."

"Leah said she thought you would have raspberries for the farm stand," Miriam said.

"I will." Rachel nodded. "And the first of the green beans, I think, as well as the last of the rhubarb."

"That is good news," Miriam said. "Leah can bring them tomorrow, if you are willing she should come."

"Of course she may come, if you truly think she can be a help."

"I do." Miriam nodded. "Though I had no idea she was so interested in the farm stand."

"Leah feels things very strongly," Rachel said. "I have cautioned her that it might be better to be more moderate, but that is not a message it is easy to hear when you are young. But Jacob understood her, I think. Leah went to see him at least once a week, and I know they had great fondness for each other. Spending time with your father was good for Leah."

"It was good for Daed, too. He looked forward to Leah's visits. He said she made him laugh."

"He had such a calm and quiet way about him, patient when others might not be," Rachel said.

"Much like you," Miriam answered with a smile. "In fact," she continued more slowly, "now that I think about it, it has always seemed to me that you and Daed were much alike."

"You think so?" Rachel asked, with something in her voice that Miriam could not quite put her finger on.

"I do." She nodded.

45

"Then I will thank you," Rachel said. "For I take that as a compliment. And you, Miriam? Is all well with you and Daniel?"

"Oh, *ja*," Miriam said quickly. "Everything is fine. Daniel is well." But her voice sounded brittle, even to her own ears, and she could feel her color rise. *Just like Leah,* she thought. Blushing under Rachel's steady gaze, though the older woman had made no comment but simply continued to regard Miriam with calm and compassionate eyes.

"It is a lot to take in, all at once," Miriam continued somewhat haltingly. "Losing Daed, and Sarah coming home. But I am as well as can be, I suppose, and as for the rest, I am trying to be patient and humble and surrender to the will of God."

All of a sudden, Miriam felt a great surge of relief flow through her. It felt so good to admit these simple truths, as if just speaking of them, acknowledging them as burdens, had somehow lifted the weight of them. As she had earlier, standing beside her mother's grave, Miriam suddenly found herself wondering what it would have been like to have had a mother, an older, more experienced woman in whom she could confide.

Rachel must be about Mamm's age, she realized.

"I am sorry that you are troubled," Rachel said. "Will it help to remember that even our troubles can be gifts from God? Learning how to carry them—and that we can carry them—can be part of *how* we learn to be truly humble, don't you find? Though of course this can be very hard. But it is a way to prove ourselves *to* ourselves, I think, even as we prove ourselves to God."

46

"I never thought about it quite that way," Miriam admitted.

"Ah, well," Rachel said, her tone gentle. "But then I have the advantage. After all, I am the bishop's wife."

The laugh bubbled up and out of Miriam before she even knew that it was there. Surprised, it was all she could do not to clap a hand over her mouth.

But Rachel did not seem offended. If anything, it was just the opposite. "There now," she said. "I have reached two decisions this morning. The first is that Leah may work at the farm stand. The second is that you should laugh more often."

"I do feel better," Miriam admitted. "Thank you, Rachel."

To her surprise, Rachel laid a gentle palm against Miriam's cheek. "You are welcome. Now I think we both should head indoors. If I know John Miller, he will be home soon and wanting his dinner."

"Oh, my goodness, dinner!" Miriam exclaimed. "Can you believe I've forgotten all about it? Though in my case, no harm done. Daniel is working with Lucas today, so he'll eat with his family."

"Well," Rachel said, "at least we both remembered in time. I will send Leah and some produce to you first thing tomorrow morning."

"I'll look forward to it," Miriam said. "Thank you again, Rachel."

Miriam turned and walked with quick steps back toward the road. With every step she took, it seemed to her that her heart felt lighter than it had in many months.

Perhaps Rachel is right, she thought. *Perhaps I should laugh more.*

Now all she had to do was to figure out how.

From the window of her upstairs bedroom, Leah watched Miriam walk swiftly down the Millers' drive. Leah had flown through setting the table for dinner, hoping against hope that the two women would call her back outside so that her *aenti* could share what she had decided about Leah working at the farm stand. That hadn't happened, though. So, after giving the table a final check to make sure everything was as it should be, Leah had dashed upstairs. Her bedroom was in the left front corner of the house, and her windows faced both front, toward the drive, and to the side, over the kitchen garden.

I'm not really spying, she thought. *I just want to see what Aenti Rachel and Miriam look like.* Were they smiling or serious? And which expression might mean that Leah would be allowed to work at the farm stand?

But being able to see her *aenti* and Miriam hadn't helped matters one single bit. As a matter of fact, the more she studied them, the more clear it became to Leah that she couldn't figure out what Aenti Rachel and Miriam were talking about at all. Miriam looked so sober and serious. *So sad,* Leah thought. Then she was laughing in the blink of an eye. But it was what happened next that caught Leah's attention and held it fast. As she watched, Aenti Rachel reached out and laid her palm against Miriam's cheek.

Now I know they're not talking about the farm stand,

she thought. And she knew something else. She knew that her aunt cared for Miriam Brennemann very much. For this was Aenti Rachel's *special gesture*, the one she used as a way of offering comfort or consolation when no words would suffice.

For as long as Leah could remember, Aenti Rachel had touched Leah's own cheek in just that fashion whenever Leah felt bad, *really* bad. Whether it was the flu she'd had just last year, the one that had left her feeling so miserable she wanted to cry like a baby, or the time she had been daydreaming while doing the dishes and let her favorite cup—the one that had once belonged to her mother and was one of the few mementos she had of her—slip from her fingers and fall to the floor, shattering into pieces too numerous to count. Leah had been horrified by the accident, too upset even to cry. She'd simply stood in the kitchen, gazing down at the shards of crockery surrounding her bare feet. She could have walked on the pieces and not bled, she had thought, her body was that numb.

And then Aenti Rachel was there, in the kitchen doorway, taking in the situation with one glance, taking charge at once.

"*Ach*, Leah!" she had softly exclaimed. "Stay still. I will clean this up."

Quickly, Aenti Rachel had retrieved the broom and dustpan and swept the shards from around Leah's feet. Then she had gone for Leah's slippers in case there were pieces of crockery too small to see that still might cut. It was as Leah braced herself, one hand on her *aenti*'s shoulder, that the words—and tears—began to flow.

"It was the only thing I had of Mamm's, and now it's gone."

"I know," Aenti Rachel said. "I know it feels that way. You treasured the cup, and I am sorry you have lost it. But you have many things of your mother's, Leah. When you are calmer, you will see."

But Leah would not be consoled. She had moved through the rest of that evening in a fog of misery, longing only for the moment when she could go to bed and close her eyes. But as she reached to turn down the lamp, her aunt had come into her room. Aenti Rachel had smoothed the coverlet, tucking Leah in just as she had done when Leah was very small. Then she leaned over and gently placed her palm against Leah's cheek, gazing steadily into her eyes.

And it was in that moment that Leah understood. She had not lost everything connected to her mother after all. In fact, she still had something far more important than any possession could ever be. She had her mother's sister, Aenti Rachel herself.

"I love you, Aenti Rachel," she had whispered.

"As I love you, *schatzi*," her aunt had replied. "Go to sleep now. Things will seem better in the morning."

Before her aunt could get up, Leah had reached to cover her aunt's hand with her own. "Things are better *now*."

Aenti Rachel was silent for many moments, so many that Leah thought she might not speak at all.

"I am glad to hear you say so," she finally said. "You are growing into a fine young woman, Leah. I believe your mother would be proud. Get a good night's sleep now. You'll have that floor to mop in the morning."

Then she turned down the lamp and left the room. Leah was smiling as she closed her eyes.

"Leah? Where have you got to?" Her aunt's voice pulled her back to the present.

"Here I am, Aenti Rachel," Leah called. "I'll be right down."

She dashed out of her bedroom and raced downstairs, clutching at the banister so that she could take the stairs two at a time. Not until she reached the bottom did she remember that her aunt had forbidden her to do that very thing. Leah slowed her pace.

"The table looks lovely, Leah," her aunt said as Leah entered the kitchen.

"Danki," Leah said at once.

"If the work you perform for Miriam is half so nice, I am sure she will be pleased," Rachel Miller went on.

"You said yes?" Leah cried.

"I said yes," her aunt confirmed. "You will start work at the Stony Field Farm Stand first thing tomorrow morning."

Five

Miriam stepped into her kitchen, still feeling lighter from the visit she'd just had with Rachel, only to find Sarah, clutching a fork and looking frantic.

"Oh, Miriam!" Sarah spun around to face her. "There you are. I overslept. I know I overslept. I'm sorry. I guess I'm still on west coast time."

She darted around to the far side of the table and set the fork in its place with a *whack*.

"You saved me some coffee. That was nice," she continued before Miriam could get a word in edgewise. "But then, when I went to the farm stand you weren't there and I didn't know where to look and then I thought it must be almost dinnertime and so then I came back here and I—"

"Sarah," Miriam said, finally halting the flow of her sister's words.

"What?"

"It's all right. Calm down."

"I am calm," Sarah protested, her tone slightly indignant. "I just didn't know what you expected me to do, that's all."

"I didn't expect you to do anything," Miriam said. "No, wait," she added quickly at the stricken look in Sarah's eyes. She crossed the room to lay a hand on her sister's shoulder. "I'm sorry," she said. "That came out wrong. I only meant you needn't have worried. I would have been home in plenty of time if we needed to fix dinner. I never meant to leave it for you to do, especially as it's just your first day here. Your first ordinary day," she added.

"But, Daniel—" Sarah faltered.

"Is helping Lucas," Miriam told her. "He'll have his dinner at his mother's table, not ours."

Miriam couldn't help but notice her sister's concern for *her* husband. Daniel talked of Sarah, and Sarah talked of Daniel. The two seemed equally matched in their concern for each other. It made Miriam feel small, as if she were disappearing out of her own life.

Still, Miriam wanted her sister's stay to be a good one. She had loved Sarah all her life, and that was what she wanted to feel in her sister's presence. Not this awful, crippling jealousy. *She's my sister. I will be loving toward her,* Miriam silently resolved.

"Oh," Sarah said, sounding distressed. She gazed down at the table.

"Sarah, what is it? What's wrong?" Miriam asked, surprised by Sarah's distress. The Sarah of her memory always seemed so confident, so self-assured. The Sarah standing beside her wasn't like that at all. Sarah was dressed in jeans and button-down shirt with a flowered print. The clothing was modest and yet seemed so out of place.

"I guess it just feels strange to be back," Sarah said, echoing Miriam's thought. "And without Daed, the house feels so . . ." She trailed off, shaking her head.

"So empty," Miriam filled in quietly. "I know. I feel that way, too."

"Empty," Sarah echoed. "That's a nicer way of putting it than what I came up with."

"What was that?"

"Wrong."

"I suppose I can see how you would feel that way," Miriam acknowledged. "But Daed's death comes from God just as his life did, Sarah. It can't be wrong."

"I know," Sarah said. "I know that. I guess I'm just having a harder time believing it than I expected." She pulled in a deep breath. "So," she went on in a deliberately brighter tone. "It's just you and me. What shall we do for our lunch?"

"How about a picnic?" Miriam suggested. "We can go out onto the porch. It's such a lovely day. There's still plenty of cold food left over from yesterday, and if we take paper plates, we won't have any washing up."

"Is there still chow-chow?" Sarah asked, her tone slightly wistful. "There's no such thing in San Francisco, unless I make it myself." She wrinkled her nose. "I've tried every type of relish they sell in that city, even at the fancy gourmet stores, and nothing even comes close."

"Where exactly do you think you are?" Miriam asked, smiling.

"Well, now, let me see," Sarah said. She regarded Miriam, her head cocked to one side. *She looks just like a bird studying a worm,* Miriam thought. "I see a woman dressed in Plain clothes with a white *kapp* on her head, and there's not an electric light switch in sight. I would say chances are very good that this *is* a Plain house."

"In that case, you're in luck," Miriam said. "There will be chow-chow."

"And pie?"

"And pie."

"Outstanding!" Sarah cried. "Though I'll have to watch myself. I could gain ten pounds in the blink of an eye. But what the heck! Bring on the paper plates!" She glanced at the wristwatch she wore and shook her head. "This will be more like breakfast for me."

"I think you're right," Miriam observed.

"About what?"

"You *are* still on west coast time."

"That was so good!" Sarah exclaimed after she swallowed the last crumb of pie crust. "Sometimes I forget how good the food from home is."

"Seeing as we've already established this is a Plain house," Miriam said, "there's plenty more where that came from."

"Oh, no," Sarah said. She pushed her paper plate to arm's length. "If I eat another bite, I think I'll explode!"

"I know what you mean," Miriam admitted. She regarded her own entirely empty plate. "I may have gotten a little carried away myself."

"You know what Daed would say is the cure for that, don't you?" Sarah said.

"I do," Miriam replied with a smile. "Just like I remember what we always *wanted* the answer to be." She caught Sarah's eye.

"A nap," the sisters said in unison, and then laughed.

After all the grief and tension of the last week, sitting on the porch and laughing with Sarah today was about the last thing Miriam would have imagined for herself. Nor could she have imagined that it would feel so good.

"We never got those naps," Sarah remembered with a sigh. "Instead, we always wound up with Daed's cure for everything—good, old-fashioned hard work."

"Ja," Miriam agreed. "I remember when I was nine and had the chicken pox and Daed seemed astonished that washing up the dishes didn't make me feel better."

"He was stubborn that way," Sarah said in a soft voice. "Do you remember how Amelia had to tell him to let you rest in bed until your fever broke? 'Jacob, you cannot expect that child to scrub a floor now.'" Sarah got the indignant pitch of Amelia's voice perfectly. "And so then *I* had to scrub it!"

It occurred to Miriam that Sarah was the only person who knew her whole life this way. No one else had shared the house with Daed; no one else had grown up with his presence. No one else would ever understand her so completely.

"Well, at least we can take doing the dishes off our list for now," Miriam said.

"Good!" Sarah said with a smile. "But I know the way things work around here. I haven't been gone that long. There's probably something we're supposed to be doing right this very minute."

"Well," Miriam said, drawing out the single syllable. Sarah chuckled. "I had planned to spend the afternoon at the farm stand," Miriam went on. "But there's a lot less to do there now, as I had some unexpected help this morning."

"But we can still go down to the stand, can't we?" Sarah asked quickly. "You didn't get everything done."

"You know what else Daed always said," Miriam answered.

Sarah sat up a little straighter in her chair, imitating their father's ramrod posture. " 'There is always something more that can be done,' " she intoned. Then she slumped, becoming herself once more. "Trouble is, he was right."

"He almost always was."

"He was, wasn't he?" Sarah agreed softly.

Both sisters fell silent, gazing out over the green fields of the farm. From this vantage, everything looked peaceful, serene, unchanging, as if the farm existed out of time and the fields simply took care of themselves. But Miriam knew the truth.

Daed was right, she thought. There *was* always something more that could be done, especially on a farm. This place had been Jacob Lapp's home and life's work for all of his days, just as it had been his father's and grandfather's before him. *And now the farm is mine,* Miriam thought. It belonged to her and Daniel. It was up to them to carry on the traditions that had come before them. Traditions that supported Miriam, that gave her life meaning. Traditions that she loved.

She stood up. "One thing's for certain," she said, "sitting here won't get anything done."

"Gracious, Miriam," Sarah said as she, too, rose. "You *do* sound just like Daed."

"Come on," Miriam said. "Let's get these plates taken care of. Then we can go down to the stand."

"I just need to put some shoes on," Sarah said. "I'm out of practice for going barefoot outdoors."

"The *Englischers* don't go barefoot?" Miriam asked. She held the kitchen door open for Sarah as the two went back into the house.

"They do," Sarah replied, "just not as often as you'd suppose, and children much more than adults. You almost never see a grown-up *Englisch* man without his shoes on, not even in a park. Though they do go barefoot on the beaches," she added. "There are even signs in stores near the beach, telling people they have to wear shoes."

Miriam found this interesting. "You mean, they have more rules than we do?"

"Just different ones," Sarah said.

"And just what were you doing going around looking at what *Englisch* men have on their feet?" Miriam inquired.

Sarah laughed. "Never you mind. Give me a minute. I'll be right back."

She sprinted up the stairs, her bare feet slapping against the wooden treads.

Quickly, Miriam put away the china plates Sarah had set out earlier, washed the silverware, and then put the paper plates and food scraps in the bucket for the compost. She would take it out to the garden compost pile after supper that night.

She was washing and drying her hands when Sarah came clattering back downstairs. "What on earth?" Miriam exclaimed as she turned toward the sound. "What did you do? Put on a pair of boots?"

"Hardly," Sarah replied. She extended one leg, the better to display the strappy platform sandals she now wore. "These are considered very fashionable, I'll have you know."

Miriam stared. "I could never walk in something like that," she murmured. "I'd break a leg."

"You wouldn't," Sarah assured her. "You get used to them."

"Honestly?"

Sarah put her hands on her hips. "Yes, honestly," she said, and Miriam thought she detected both laughter and exasperation in her sister's voice. "Don't you ever go into any of the shoe stores in town?"

"Not to look for shoes like that, I don't. They would be next to useless on a farm."

How could Sarah even ask such a foolish question? Surely she hadn't forgotten that much about Plain life.

Sarah sighed. "Never mind. I'm ready to head to the farm stand if you are."

"I'm ready," Miriam said.

Together, the sisters left the house. They walked in silence, the hard soles of Sarah's shoes crunching against the gravel of the drive.

"I didn't mean to offend you," Miriam finally said. "It's just—I can't imagine—"

"I know," Sarah said, cutting off Miriam's halting words. "I'm being foolish, Miriam, and I'm sorry for it. I just feel so out of sorts. I knew that I would feel sad, but I didn't expect the rest, I guess. I didn't expect to feel so much like a stranger, a foreigner."

Miriam was silent.

"Thank you," Sarah said after a moment.

"What for?"

"For not trying to tell me I'm not a stranger, I suppose."

"I'll tell you the truth," Miriam said, though she sent an inquiring glance in her sister's direction. Sarah nodded, as if to tell Miriam to go ahead. "I'm not sure I know what you are."

"That makes us even, then," Sarah answered. "Though," she went on quickly, "when I'm out among the *Englischers* I feel as if I know, at least most of the time."

"Why did you stay away so long?" Miriam hadn't meant to ask. The question, which she had wondered about for so long, just seemed to emerge on its own.

"A lot of reasons," Sarah said. "I haven't had much time when I could leave. School was nonstop, and then I started my job the same week I graduated. My job, it's working with troubled kids. That is, kids who don't have strong families or even enough food. They need help all the time. It's hard to take time away from them. Also, though I work long hours, I'm not paid a lot and San Francisco is an expensive city to live in. For a long time, I didn't have enough money for a flight."

"But you had enough for this trip?"

"I've been saving a little from every paycheck for two years now. So, yes, I finally had enough."

The sisters fell silent once more. They came to the end of the long drive and turned onto the road, and the farm stand came into view.

"Do you remember how Daed came up with the name for the stand?" Sarah asked, abruptly changing the subject.

"Of course I do," Miriam said with a smile. "He said he plowed up so many rocks to clear the land for it, there was only one choice."

"Stony Field Farm Stand," Sarah said. She and Miriam reached the back door. "You keep it locked now," Sarah went on. "I noticed that when I came down earlier."

"Daed decided it would be best." Miriam put the key into the padlock, twisted to open it, and then slipped the padlock off the door. "There was some vandalism a year or so ago. Somebody went around making mischief all over the county. They never did figure out who it was. So Daed decided we should lock the doors to the farm stand, since it's so close to the road. I don't think he ever really liked doing it, though."

She stepped across the threshold, fingers going unerringly to the switch for the overhead lights. The interior of the stand felt close and warm, though Miriam had closed it up no more than an hour or so before. She threaded her way through the stand to open the doors at the front, just as she had that morning. Afternoon sunshine streamed in, followed by a quick, fresh breeze.

"There now," Sarah said. "This feels just right."

"Really?" Miriam asked in surprise. "I would have thought—" She stopped short, biting the tip of her tongue.

"What?" Sarah inquired.

"It's just that I associate the stand so much with Daed." Miriam faltered. "He spent almost all his time here toward the end, when he couldn't work in the fields at all. I was going to say that this was one of the places that seems most empty without him, but then I thought—"

"You thought there was no way I'd feel the way you do," Sarah filled in, "because I wasn't there at the end. But you think I should have been. You think I was wrong to go. You've always thought so."

"I didn't say that," Miriam protested.

"That doesn't mean you don't think it," Sarah answered shortly. "You've never understood why I felt I had to leave. Admit it."

"All right, maybe I haven't," Miriam said. "But that's not the same as saying I think it was wrong for you to go."

If you hadn't gone, I might never have married Daniel, she thought. But she knew she could never say such a thing aloud.

"I don't know very much about your life," she went on slowly. "You've only been home twice in six years, until now. And you don't really talk about life among the *Englischers* much when you're here, not to me anyhow. I didn't think you wanted to talk about it—at least not to me."

"That's not true. What do you want to know? Just ask," Sarah said.

"Everything. Nothing. How should I know?" Miriam exclaimed, throwing up her hands. "Sarah, I don't want us to quarrel. I'm not even sure how we got into this conversation in the first place."

"Neither am I," Sarah said. "I'm sorry." She huffed out

a breath that was not quite a laugh. "I seem to be saying that a lot today . . . And if you tell me an apology never hurts, I'll think you've actually turned into Daed, so just don't."

"Well, it doesn't," Miriam said. She bit down on her bottom lip to hold back a smile.

"I know," Sarah replied. "I probably know it better than you do, in fact. I was the one who did most of the apologizing when we were growing up, as I recall."

"What was it Berthe Meyer always used to call you?" Miriam asked.

"High-spirited," Sarah answered with a snort of laughter. She gave a theatrical shudder. "Berthe Meyer. Don't remind me."

"Sorry," Miriam said, then clapped a hand across her mouth as Sarah's laughter rang out, full-blown. "I did *not* do that on purpose," Miriam said, as she felt her own laughter bubble up. "It just popped out!"

"Guess Berthe still brings out the worst in both of us."

"Sarah," Miriam protested, but she was laughing herself now.

Berthe Meyer was the most outspoken woman in the district. She'd been known to try even Bishop John's patience. She had not approved of Jacob Lapp raising two young girls on his own. As a result, she had seldom approved of Miriam and Sarah and hadn't hesitated to say so.

"Enough of this nonsense!" Sarah said, with a stamp of one foot. "It makes me giddy. Give me something to do so I can settle down."

"There's not much left," Miriam admitted. She put her hands on her hips and turned in a slow circle, gazing at the farm stand's interior. "We could take stock of the jams and canned goods, I suppose. Those are always big sellers among the *Englischers* and I don't want to run out."

"Counting canned goods," Sarah repeated. "Sounds perfect for me."

"Take this," Miriam said. She reached beneath the cash register, opened a drawer, and brought out a notebook. "It should tell you who brought in what and how many of each kind. If we're down to two jars of anything, write it down. Then I can speak with whoever it is on Sunday to see if she has more that she'd like to bring us."

"Pen? Pencil?" Sarah asked.

"Here," Miriam said, fetching a pen from the same drawer. "Sometimes we keep extra preserves on the top shelves," she added. "You should check there, too. You'll probably need the stepladder for that."

"Okay." Sarah nodded and got to work. Miriam stood for a moment, uncertain of what she should do herself. As Miriam stood hesitating, Sarah picked up a jar of strawberry jam and lifted it up toward the sunlight. "These look so good!" she said. "I'm not surprised the *Englischers* buy so many."

"Don't they ever make any of their own?"

This was a question Miriam had always wanted to ask, but it seemed rude to ask any of her *Englisch* customers.

"Some do." Sarah nodded. "It used to be considered kind of old-fashioned, but lately it's sort of—I don't know—come back into style."

"Style?" Miriam echoed.

Sarah laughed. "You expect the *Englischers* to make the

same sense you do," she observed. "That's not going to get you very far."

"How did you ever get used to living among them?" Miriam asked. "Wasn't it hard?"

"It was, at first," Sarah acknowledged. "Actually, it still is, sometimes." She set the jar back on the shelf and turned to face Miriam more fully. "There are so many people in San Francisco, Miriam! I'd never seen so many before. And all so different from one another, not like the people here at all."

"We're not all the same," Miriam protested.

"No," Sarah agreed. "Of course not. But you all agree to abide by the *Ordnung*, or at least you agree to try. That's part of what becoming Plain means, isn't it? It's part of what keeps you separate from everyone else. Right?"

"Yes." Miriam nodded. "I can see your point."

You, she thought. *She says* you, *not* we. *Not anymore.*

"Take the clothing, for example," Sarah went on. "All the women here wear similar dresses—different colors maybe, but very similar. And all the women and girls wear *kapps*. But the *Englischers*, most of them anyhow, don't want that at all. They want to be unique individuals, not part of a crowd. You've seen the fashions on the tourists. The women might wear skirts or dresses or jeans or shorts. They use their clothing to distinguish themselves, to make themselves different and attractive."

"But—" Miriam said, then stopped.

"No, go on," Sarah said.

"How can anyone live like that? How do you know who you are?"

"Those are good questions," Sarah admitted. "And they're ones a lot of people struggle with. Not just people like me. Lots of *Englischers* struggle with them as well. But do you want to know something funny?" Sarah went on with a smile. "The things I struggled with the most, at first anyhow, weren't anything so profound. There were just so many things to *do*, Miriam! Wonderful things like museums and libraries, even simply walking around. Some days, I got dizzy just thinking about them. Others, I ended up doing nothing at all because I couldn't decide what to do first! And then there was the noise."

Sarah shook her head. "I'm still not used to that, to tell you the truth. It still catches me off guard sometimes. Cars honking and buses roaring up and down the streets, radios blaring, people walking down the street talking on their cell phones. It's like you can almost *see* the sound. When I first started school, I used to lie in bed in my dorm room at night, trying to re-create in my mind the silence of my old room at home."

"And could you?" Miriam asked, fascinated in spite of herself.

"I could," Sarah said. "Right up until the moment my roommate started snoring."

"Oh, no!"

"Oh, yes," Sarah said with a grin. "The first night it happened, I almost cried. But I'd promised myself I would never do that, so . . ."

A sharp trilling sound, like the ring of an old-fashioned phone, cut through the air of the farm stand. Both sisters jumped.

"What on earth?" Miriam exclaimed.

But Sarah was busy digging her fingers into the back pocket of her jeans and pulling out a slim, brightly colored phone. She glanced at the front.

"It's work; I have to take this," she said, as she checked the number. She set the pen and notebook on the counter beside the cash register. "I'll be right back. Sorry."

She put an index finger to the front of the phone, then swiftly moved the phone to her ear.

"Hello, this is Sarah Lapp," she said as she stepped outside.

Miriam shook her head with an inward smile. There was Sarah complaining about the city's noise, and her own cell phone went off, as if she were importing the din to Lancaster. Miriam found herself grateful that she and Daniel didn't have cell phones and the only nearby pay phone was in Daniel's father's barn.

She picked up the pen and notebook Sarah had abandoned, determined to finish the job herself. Abruptly a wave of weariness swept over her.

It can wait until tomorrow, she thought. Taking stock would be a good task for Leah, a good way to introduce her to some of the inner workings of the farm stand.

Miriam leaned her arms on the counter, gazing out the front doors. *Why am I so tired?* she wondered. The day was only just half done, and she had hardly done anything, not by her usual standards.

I guess I'm still getting used to life without Daed, she thought.

She straightened up. *I'll spend some time in the garden,*

she decided. Tending the kitchen garden had always been one of her favorite activities. She didn't even mind pulling the weeds, not that she allowed many to take hold. She tended garden too well for that.

Feeling better now that she had a definite purpose, Miriam closed up the farm stand and locked the back door behind her. She could see Sarah, a ways down the drive. She was pacing back and forth, speaking animatedly into the cell phone.

That looks serious, Miriam thought. Could there be trouble at Sarah's job? *I don't even really know what it is she does,* Miriam realized.

Sarah was right. She *did* seem like a stranger.

Is that what we feel like to her? Miriam wondered. But what she really wanted to know was . . . did Daniel feel that way about Sarah?

This was a possibility that Miriam had never considered before. The Sarah who was here, today, no longer matched the Sarah of Miriam's memory, the one she conjured up in her mind's eye. Did Daniel feel this way as well? If he did, would it bring him closer to Miriam, who was so close and so familiar? Or would the new Sarah seem even more interesting? Next to Sarah, would Miriam seem drab and dull?

Suddenly, the sky seemed to darken as Miriam walked to her empty house alone.

Six

Miriam was halfway to her house when she saw a small figure dashing toward her.

"Miriam! Miriam!" an exuberant voice called.

It was Daniel's youngest brother, ten-year-old Matthew, pelting down the drive as fast as his bare feet could carry him. Unless Miriam missed her guess, he had run all the way from the Brennemann farm. Though both the Lapp and Brennemann farms had many acres to their names, the farmhouses had been set so as to be reasonably close together, the country equivalent of side by side. Family members could get from one farmhouse to the other by cutting across a great open meadow. There was no need to go all the way to the main road. But, like the farm stand and the Lapp farmhouse, the Lapp and Brennemann farmhouses were hidden from each other by the gently rolling hills that dominated the countryside.

Miriam didn't think she had ever met a boy who loved to run as much as Matthew Brennemann did. His mother, Amelia, always claimed it was because he was doing his best to catch up to his four older brothers. Considering that the twins, Jonas and Joshua, the next closest in age, were seventeen, Miriam didn't think Matthew was going to slow down anytime soon.

"Hello, Matthew," she said with a smile. She stopped walking, standing still in the center of the drive while Matthew ran a great circle around her. "Are you well?" she asked. "Is everything all right at the farm?"

"Ja," Matthew panted.

He completed one more circuit then skidded to a stop in front of Miriam, his chest rising and falling with his quick breaths in and out. He looked like he belonged on one of the postcards the *Englischers* were always asking to buy, Miriam thought. Matthew's hair was as pale as corn silk. A smattering of freckles raced across his nose and cheekbones. In his dark pants, sky blue shirt, and dark suspenders, he was the perfect image of a Plain child.

"Mamm asks, will you and your sister please come to supper," Matthew went on. "She's making chicken and dumplings. They're Daniel's favorite, and mine, too, so you should say yes."

"Of course I will say yes," Miriam replied with a smile. "And I'll tell you a secret: Chicken and dumplings are my favorites, too."

"Hooray!" Matthew shouted. As if her acceptance had

been the secret signal for the start of the next race, Matthew began to run once more. He shot past Miriam, arms outstretched like airplane wings. He made a wide, banking turn before heading back across the fields toward home. "I will tell Mamm," he called over his shoulder as he went by. "Don't be late or all the dumplings will be gone!"

"I will not be late," Miriam called back.

She turned and began to walk home briskly, all her earlier weariness gone. Next to her own home, the farm where Daniel had grown up was Miriam's favorite place on earth, always filled with the joy and laughter of family life. And the seriousness, too, Miriam acknowledged. Nobody could raise seven children without encountering life's ups and downs.

What was the phrase the *Englischer* man who had stopped at the farm stand a couple of weeks ago had used? She could still see him in her mind's eye, red faced and perspiring. His car had broken down several miles down the road and, for some reason Miriam could not now recall, he'd been without a cell phone. He had stopped at the farm stand, assuming he could call from there, and had been taken aback when Jacob explained that the closest phone was a pay phone in the Brennemanns' barn.

A walk in the park. That was it, Miriam thought. *He said life's not always a walk in the park.* She remembered how the pronouncement had made her father smile. "Nope, not always a walk in the park," the man had said, "but that doesn't mean you can't stop to smell the roses." When Miriam had protested that they had no roses, the man had given Daed a wink. "So I see," he'd replied. "Guess I'll just have to settle for that basket of tomatoes instead."

She had felt foolish at the time. But now she thought she could see what the *Englisch* man had meant. You could not always predict what life would bring, but you could always try to make the best of it.

Supper with Daniel's family might be just what Miriam needed to chase away her dark thoughts.

I must take something to Amelia, she thought. Something that would express Miriam's appreciation for being asked to supper. Something to celebrate both the sweetness and the hard work of family life. Her mind busy with just what this might be, Miriam continued on toward the house.

"Your blackberry jam," Amelia Brennemann exclaimed that evening as Miriam handed her a basket with several jars nestled inside. She had tucked a clean white dish towel around them to keep them from being jostled too hard. "Oh, Miriam, you shouldn't have, but I won't say no! Do you know, no matter how many jars of jam I make, I never seem to make enough. I don't know where the boys put it."

"Hollow legs," Miriam suggested with a smile.

She stepped across the threshold and into the kitchen. As was the case in Miriam's own home, visitors used the front door only for formal occasions. It was the kitchen that was really the heart of the farmhouse. At the moment, the room was filled with the good smells of the summer supper they were all about to enjoy. Amelia's oldest daughter, fifteen-year-old Elizabeth, was putting the finishing touches on setting the big kitchen table, which was spread with a fresh oilcloth. Lucas's wife, Annaliese, was keeping an eye on the stove. Her three-year-old daughter, Jane, was right beside her, clutching at her legs, her dark eyes huge as she regarded the newcomers.

"Look who is here, Jane," Annaliese said as she sent Miriam a warm smile. Annaliese had grown up in a nearby district. She and Lucas had met when Annaliese had attended the wedding of a cousin. They had been married the next winter, just a year after Miriam and Daniel. Miriam and Annaliese had liked each other at once. "Miriam has come."

"Miriam!" Jane crowed. Miriam knelt and opened her arms. The child catapulted into them. Miriam lifted her up, burying her face in the crook of Jane's neck. She breathed in the child's sweet scent.

"You smell like sunshine, Jane," she said, trying to ignore the fierce ache of longing that had suddenly reared up to grab her by the throat.

"Outside!" Jane demanded.

Miriam gave her nose a tweak. "Not now. Now we are getting ready for supper. Are those hands clean? Let me see."

Obediently, Jane extended her hands, palms facing up. Miriam leaned closer, her face almost in Jane's hands. The child chortled at this.

"Well, they *look* clean," Miriam admitted. "But I'll tell you what. I need to wash mine. How would it be if you helped me with that? That way, we can make sure yours are clean, too."

Jane gave an enthusiastic nod. "Jane is a good helper," she informed Miriam.

"Jane!" Annaliese protested even as Miriam laughed.

"Now, where did you hear that?" she inquired. With the child still held tightly in her arms, Miriam moved toward the kitchen sink with its small hand pump. Clearly accustomed to the routine, Jane leaned over and held out her hands.

"But where is Sarah?" Amelia asked.

"Here I am," Sarah said. She stood, hesitating, just inside the kitchen door.

"Don't just stand there, *schatzi*. Come inside and let me get a good look at you."

"Amelia," Sarah said.

Even occupied as she was, Miriam heard the catch in Sarah's voice. She looked up quickly and thought she caught the bright sheen of tears in her sister's eyes. Sarah had changed from her jeans to a blue calf-length skirt with the same flowered shirt.

"Gracious!" Amelia exclaimed. "What are they feeding you out among the *Englischers*? You've grown so tall!"

"It's the shoes," Miriam said.

"Shoes!" Jane shouted.

"Jane," Annaliese said reprovingly, though Miriam heard the thread of laughter in her tone. "Inside voices in the house."

"No, no," Sarah said with a slightly watery laugh. She dashed a quick hand across her eyes. "I hate to admit it, but Miriam is right." She extended one foot to show Annaliese her shoe.

"Oh, my goodness," Amelia said as she got a good look at the platform sandals Sarah wore. "Sarah, have you left your common sense by the side of the road? You'll break your neck, walking around here in shoes like that."

"Better not let Elizabeth see them." It was Daniel's voice. He materialized in the doorway, his broad shoulders filling up the space. Lucas was right behind him. Unless Miriam very much missed her guess, they had both done their washing up at the pump in the yard, just as they had when they were boys. "She'll want a pair and her *rumspringa* isn't 'til next year."

"Daniel!" his sister protested. Her cheeks flamed bright red, but she looked at the shoes, Miriam noticed.

"Daniel!" Jane said. She began to squirm in Miriam's embrace. Daniel moved to Miriam's side. He chucked Jane under the chin and she gave a squeal of delighted laughter. Miriam turned and placed the child into her husband's waiting arms.

Daniel lifted Jane up into the air, then angled her downward so that her feet were aimed into empty space and her forehead touched Daniel's own. To Miriam's astonishment, the child fell silent, her dark eyes gazing into Daniel's bright blue ones. A wave of emotion swept over Miriam, powerful enough to make her dizzy. She laid a hand on Daniel's arm to steady herself.

Miriam's breath caught in her throat. In that moment, it seemed to her that her entire being narrowed down to the place where her fingers curled around Daniel's arm. It seemed to her that she could feel the rush of blood through Daniel's veins, hear the beating of his heart. And through it all, woven so tightly throughout Daniel's being that it could not be separated out, it seemed to Miriam that she felt something else.

Love.

Love for the child he held in his strong and capable hands. Longing for a child of his own body, one he and Miriam could call their very own. And it was the same, the very same, as the longing that ran inside Miriam's own blood, moving through every corner of her being with each and every beat of her own heart. Miriam flushed abruptly, unbearably warm. Spots danced before her eyes.

"Miriam?" Daniel murmured.

"Here, let me take the little one." Annaliese materialized behind Miriam. Daniel lifted Jane over Miriam's shoulder to hand her to her mother. Miriam's hand slipped from Daniel's arm. She blinked, as if she'd been asleep on her feet and had suddenly awakened. Her vision cleared. Daniel made a motion, as if to reach for her, but Miriam was already shifting back, desperate to regain her balance in more ways than one. Daniel's hand dropped to his side.

"When's supper? I'm hungry!" Matthew flew into the kitchen as though he'd been fired from a slingshot, banging the screen door behind him. "I told Miriam not to be late or else I'd . . ." He caught sight of Sarah and pulled up short. "Is that—"

"Miriam's sister, Sarah? *Ja*," Daniel interrupted smoothly. He turned from Miriam to catch his youngest brother by the back of his shirt collar, tugging him backward, gently, until Matthew bumped into the front of Daniel's legs.

"Mind your manners, now. Is that how you welcome a guest to your home?"

"She's not a guest. She's Miriam's sister. You just said so," Matthew protested. He squirmed, trying unsuccessfully to escape from Daniel's grasp. "That makes her family, doesn't it?"

"*Ja,*" a new voice agreed. "That is so."

"Martin," Sarah said as Daniel's father came into the kitchen. Just as his sons had, he came in from the yard. Sarah moved to him, giving Matthew's hair a quick ruffle as she passed by. She extended her hand and Martin took it gently, engulfing it within his own. "It is so good to see you."

Martin smiled. "And you." He angled his head, his expression puzzled. "When did you grow so tall?"

"I didn't," Sarah admitted with a laugh. "It's my shoes. I had no idea they'd be the topic of so much conversation! Maybe I should just take them off."

"No time for that," Amelia announced. "It is time to eat." She put her hands on her hips and gazed around the kitchen. "Where are those boys?"

"Here we are, Mamm," Jonas said, as he and Joshua came in from outdoors. At seventeen, the twins were tall and gangly and still a little shy. Both had been baptized at the end of their *rumspringa* year, but neither was yet courting for a wife. Thirteen-year-old Hannah was hard on their heels. She carried a sturdy garden basket over one arm.

"Come, come." Amelia made a beckoning motion with her hands. "Stop dawdling, *mei kinder.* Sit down and eat before the food gets cold. Set down those vegetables, Hannah, and put Jane into her high chair while Annaliese helps me get the food on the table."

It was like a great dance, Miriam thought. With all the

bodies in motion in the kitchen, surely one would bump into another. Someone's elbow would be jostled or somebody would step on someone else's toes and the food would go flying. But somehow, it never happened. There was a stop, a start, a quick step this way or that, and suddenly everyone was seated at the table, right where they belonged.

And throughout it all, Miriam noticed the way Lucas's eyes looked for Annaliese. When they alighted on her, the expression in them was almost like a touch. Annaliese met her husband's gaze, the color rising in her face. Annaliese quickly looked away, but Miriam could see the smile hovering at the corners of her mouth.

They are so in love! she thought. So much in love it was impossible to hide. *What do people see when they look at me and Daniel?* Miriam wondered suddenly, and then wondered if she really wanted to know.

"Miriam? What wool are you gathering?" Amelia asked.

"None worth spinning," Miriam answered as she made her lips curve up into a smile. She would not infect the warmth of this family gathering with the chill of her fears. She moved toward the table.

"Sit here, Miriam," Matthew said. He patted the chair beside him. "I saved you a spot."

"*Danki*, Matthew," Miriam said. She slid in between Matthew and Annaliese, trying not to stare across the table to where Daniel and Lucas now had Sarah wedged between them, their shoulders almost close enough to touch. Usually in Plain households the men sat on one side of the table, the women on the other, but years ago, Amelia had relaxed that particular rule with her family and the Lapps, whom she also considered family.

Martin Brennemann, at the head of the table, bowed his head to say a silent grace, and they all did the same. Miriam bowed her head and closed her eyes and let the words of a simple blessing move through her.

I do give thanks, she thought. *For so very much.*

But giving thanks was not the same as saying she never felt want, she thought. What Miriam felt was not bodily hunger, however. It was a hunger of the heart.

"Miriam?" she heard Annaliese murmur quietly.

Miriam's eyes flew open. "I'm sorry," she said. "I guess I got lost in my prayers."

"It must be such a blessing to have Sarah home," her sister-in-law said with a smile. Her eyes strayed across the table to where Sarah sat between Daniel and Lucas. Sarah was reaching for a dish of green beans, and Daniel was holding it just out of reach. He passed it to Lucas over the top of Sarah's head.

"*Ja,* it is—" Miriam began but stopped, relieved, when Amelia's voice rose above the others.

"*Kinder,*" Amelia said, trying without success to make her voice sound stern. "The dinner table is no place for bad behavior."

"There are places for bad behavior?" Matthew piped up at once. "Where are they?"

"There? You see?" Amelia said, failing to hide a smile.

"There are no places for bad behavior," Lucas admitted as he set the dish of green beans in front of Sarah. His blue eyes were laughing as he looked across the table at his youngest brother, though it was clear he was making an effort to keep his expression sober. "Can you tell me why?"

"Because no place is hidden from God," Matthew answered at once.

"Ja." Lucas nodded. "That is so. No place is hidden. You cannot keep secrets from God."

With a bite of chicken and dumplings halfway to her mouth, Miriam let her fork drop to her plate with a *thunk*. She had never thought of it in quite that way, but Lucas was right. You could not keep secrets from God.

"Is something the matter, Miriam?" Amelia asked.

Miriam shook her head. She had to stop letting everything upset her. She had been off balance all day long.

"No," she said. "Of course not. To tell you the truth, I think I got greedy and took too big a bite."

"Don't worry," Matthew consoled her. "I do that all the time. Sometimes I burn my tongue."

"That's what I was trying to avoid," Miriam said. She cut into the piece of chicken and put it into her mouth quickly.

"Tell us about life among the *Englischers*, Sarah!" Elizabeth suddenly burst out, as if she'd been holding it in ever since Sarah had come through the door but could contain it no longer.

"Oh, yes," Hannah seconded. "Please tell us. Does everybody really have a cell phone? Would a girl my age have one?"

"Girls," Amelia warned. "You must not pester Sarah. She is our guest."

Sarah laughed. "Oh, I don't mind. I'm used to questions, in fact, though usually it's the other way around. When they find out I was raised here, all the *Englischers* want to know about life among the Amish." She accented the word "Amish" because the word was used only by the *Englischers*. Her head swiveled between Martin and Amelia. "But perhaps you would prefer it if I did not speak of the *Englischers*."

"No," Martin said quietly. "We do not mind. It is good to have questions answered. That way, when you make a decision you know it is the right one."

"You sound just like my father," Sarah said.

"Jacob was a fine man and a good friend," Martin Brennemann answered.

"To answer your questions," Sarah continued, turning back to the girls, "I would say that most girls your age would have a cell phone, Elizabeth, and some your age would, too, Hannah. Certainly they would want one! But it would depend on how the girl's family felt about it. Though many would say yes, I think."

"Tsk," Amelia said. "So many distractions."

"For some," Sarah acknowledged. She hesitated, as if uncertain about whether or not to go on. "What you must understand is that the *Englischers want* to be connected. Sometimes I think they want to be connected to as many things as possible! They hate the thought of missing something important."

"But surely they *do* miss something important." Annaliese's voice was quiet, but she was instantly the focus of all eyes. "How can you know who you are with so much confusion? How can you hear the voice of God?"

Sarah's face lit up, as if Annaliese had asked precisely the questions she had been waiting for. "That's exactly what I wanted to know," she said. "It's part of why I decided to study social work. I wanted to see if I could find the answers to those questions—and to see if I could help."

"Help?" Amelia echoed. "Help how?"

"I work with young people," Sarah answered. "What the *Englischers* call 'troubled youth.' To put it simply, I—we—the program I now work for—we try to show the young people the way out of trouble by giving them responsibility and teaching them new skills."

"What kind of skills?" Annaliese asked.

Sarah smiled. "We teach them how to grow a garden."

Annaliese's dark eyes widened. *"What?"*

Sarah's smile became a full-blown laugh. "It's true. Many of the young people we serve come from the inner city. There's no room for a patch of grass where they live, let alone a garden. But learning to grow a garden can teach many things. You have to be thoughtful—to plan ahead—and of course there is also the fun of choosing what you will grow. Then, after the seeds are planted, you must learn to be patient and careful. If you don't water, what will happen, Matthew?"

"That's easy," Matthew said with a snort. "Nothing."

Sarah nodded. "That's right. So then what?"

Matthew took a bite of dumpling, chewing as he considered.

"You start over?"

"That's right, too." Sarah nodded. "You start over. But what if, in the meantime, the boy in the plot next to yours has done everything just the way he should? How does that make you feel?"

Matthew's brow furrowed. "I would want to help him?"

"Maybe you would," Sarah said. "But not everyone would feel that way. Some people don't like to feel like they are failing while the guy next to them succeeds."

"I think that I begin to see the point of this," Amelia acknowledged. "And the *Englischers* pay you to do this work?"

"Not much!" Sarah admitted with a laugh. "But, yes. It's a brand-new program, in fact, and I guess you would say that I help to run it. We have an overall director, but I am the one who works most closely with the young people in the garden."

She looked down at her plate, as if concerned she would appear to be prideful. "I feel very honored and excited to be given such a job."

"Of course you do," Daniel said, scooting back his chair a little and angling his body so that he could look Sarah in the face. Miriam's eyes fixed on the picture they made together. "But why did I never hear your *daed* speak of this?"

Sarah bit her lip. "He did not know of it. He knew I was studying social work, of course, but I hadn't yet told him about the job. It was selfish of me, I admit, but I . . ." Sarah paused and took a breath, as if mustering the courage to go on. "I wanted to tell him in person, so I decided to wait until I came home. I was planning to come anyway at the end of the summer, remember?"

She glanced across the table at Miriam, and Miriam nodded.

"But then Daed died and I . . ." Sarah's voice trailed off.

Into the silence that followed her words came the shrill ringing of what Miriam now recognized as her sister's cell phone.

Sarah jumped up, as if she'd been jabbed by a needle, her face flushing scarlet.

"I'm sorry," she said. She scooted back from the table quickly, the legs of her chair making a harsh scraping sound against the floor. "I'm so sorry. It must be my job. They're the only ones who would call. Please excuse me."

She stood and, phone still shrilling, dashed out the kitchen door. But she took the time to close it gently, Miriam noticed. The sound of the phone ringing ceased the moment Sarah was outside.

"Gracious," Amelia said after a moment.

"I'm sorry," Miriam apologized also. What had Sarah been thinking, she wondered, to bring a cell phone into the Brennemanns' home? It was one thing to have one at their own house, but to bring it with you when you came to visit . . .

"She had a call earlier today, while we were working at the farm stand," Miriam continued. "It was work then, too."

"Well," Martin said, "let us hope that there is nothing wrong. I will have some more green beans, if you please."

Lucas lifted the dish of beans and passed it to his father. "Daniel says he is thinking of looking for a new horse when we go to auction, Daed."

"Ach, ja?" Martin replied. "What kind?"

Out of the corner of her eye, Miriam saw Elizabeth lift a bite of food to her mouth. Slowly but surely, the meal was getting back to normal.

"A new field horse, Daed," Daniel replied. "There is

plenty of room in the barn. I am thinking that we all would benefit from having another horse."

"Ja." Martin nodded. "That is so." He looked at his sons, his blue eyes twinkling. "Not only that, it gives all three of us a very good reason to go to the auction."

"Lucas needs a reason?" Annaliese said, her eyes deliberately wide.

"I am *so* sorry," Sarah said as she came back through the kitchen door. She sounded slightly breathless, as she had been pacing around the yard for the duration of her call. "I should have asked before I brought my phone into your home."

"Do not make too much of it, *schatzi*," Amelia said. "There was no real harm done. Nothing is too bad at this new job of yours, I hope."

Sarah shook her head as she resumed her seat. "Not really, no. But the only way I could get extra time off was to promise to be on call. One of our boys is acting out a bit now that I am gone. He isn't bad, not really," Sarah went on quickly. "He is just more troubled than some of the others. He listens to me, but he doesn't really like to listen to anybody else. Since I left, he has decided to push against the boundaries. They called to see if I would talk to him."

"So, you are good at this new job of yours," Martin observed.

Sarah sent him a grateful look. "I hope so." All of a sudden, her expression changed. "Oh, my goodness!" she exclaimed. "That reminds me. I can't believe I forgot. Speaking of needing to help . . ." She looked across the table at Miriam. "Victor King stopped by this morning while you were out."

87

"Victor King," Miriam echoed. The King farm was several miles along the same road as the Lapp and Brennemann farms. "He came to see me and not Daniel? What did he want?"

"It was to do with the farm stand," Sarah explained.

"Mei kinder," Amelia said briskly as the voices of the younger children were growing louder. "Are you finished with your meal? If so, you may spend the rest of this fine night out of doors. Annaliese and I will see to the washing up."

"Indeed you will not," Miriam put in at once. "Sarah and I will do that." She smiled at Elizabeth, Hannah, and the twins. "But I agree. It is such a fine night. The young people should be out of doors."

"May I take Jane, Annaliese?" Hannah asked, as she pushed back her chair.

"Of course. Just try not to let her get too dirty, will you? She had a bath just this afternoon and I would prefer not to have to give her another one."

"Danki, I will be careful," Hannah promised.

She plucked Jane from the high chair and settled her on one hip. There was a flurry of activity as chairs were scooted away from the table, then pushed carefully back in, and dishes were carried to the sink for washing. Matthew shot out the kitchen door with the same energy that he'd come in with.

"That one has only one speed, I see," Sarah remarked.

Amelia laughed. "Oh, no. I believe he can go faster than that. Forgive me, Sarah. I did not mean to interrupt you before, but I could see the young ones getting restless. You were talking about Victor King?"

"Ja." Miriam turned back to her sister. "Why did Victor want to see me?"

"He has a . . . situation, I guess you could say," Sarah replied. "And he wondered if the solution might be of help to you as well. His younger brother, Eli, has recently come to stay." She glanced around the table. "Though you all know that, of course. Victor wondered if you needed extra help at the farm stand and, if so, if you would be willing to take Eli on."

"Eli King wants to work at the farm stand?" Miriam echoed. All of a sudden, her brain felt slow, as if she were trying to do a puzzle but was missing some vital piece. Though she knew Victor well, she had met Eli only once, a few weeks earlier, when he had first arrived. He had come to stay with Victor from his parents' house somewhere in the Midwest, Miriam recalled. She couldn't quite remember why, but she thought there had been trouble of some kind.

"To tell you the truth," Sarah said, "I don't know what Eli wants, and neither does Victor. I think that's just the problem. Victor says his brother is at loose ends." Sarah's brow furrowed. "He's hurt his leg and can't work in the fields? Am I getting this right?" Her head swiveled between Daniel and Lucas.

"Ja." Daniel nodded. "There was an accident, back home. Buggy racing, I think John Miller said it was, though I don't think this is widely known. Eli was injured, and another boy as well. Eli's mother is a widow with a houseful of children to raise, all on her own now. I think she was hoping that having an older man around the house would

be good for Eli. Help to settle him down. Since his father's death, he's grown a little wild."

"So Victor wants his wild younger brother to work at the farm stand?" Miriam asked. "He wants me to be responsible for him?"

"But that's a great idea!" Sarah cried, her voice riding right over Miriam's.

Miriam stared across the table at her younger sister, struggling to contain her rising annoyance and dismay.

"What's so great about it?" she inquired.

"It will give him responsibility and focus, don't you see?" Sarah answered promptly. "The same things we try to give the kids I work with in San Francisco. Victor's right, really. It's an excellent solution to both your problem and his."

In spite of her best efforts, Miriam felt her hold on her temper slipping. "I didn't know I had a *problem*."

But Sarah seemed oblivious. She shifted in her chair to face Daniel. "Don't you think so?"

"Decisions about the farm stand are really Miriam's to make," Daniel said, his voice cautious. He glanced across the table at Miriam, and then turned his attention back to Sarah. "But I must confess I think the idea seems a sound one."

"But I already have help," Miriam protested as, finally, her brain provided the perfect counterargument. "Leah Gingerich, Rachel Miller's niece, came to the farm stand today. She has asked if she might help me. Bishop John and Rachel have given their permission, and I have already said yes."

She looked across the table at Daniel, willing him to

meet her eyes. "I am sorry to spring this on you as a surprise, but there simply hasn't been time to tell you."

"But that's even better," Sarah said. "I can help while I'm here, but that will only be until the end of the summer, when I have to go back. If you take on Eli, you'll still have two helpers when I leave, not just one."

Miriam held her breath. Now would be the time, she thought. The time for Daniel to speak up and support her, his wife.

"The decision is Miriam's to make," Daniel said once more, and Miriam felt herself start to relax. Then Daniel went on, "But I must admit that what Sarah says makes sense to me. Having Eli come to work at the farm stand could be a good thing for all. And there is no reason why he and Leah cannot work together."

Sarah actually clapped her hands. "So that's settled, then," she said. She looked across the table at Miriam. "Right?"

No, it's not.

The thought was so loud and clear in Miriam's mind that for a moment she feared she had spoken it aloud.

But no one at the table seemed to think anything was amiss. No one except Miriam. And she knew exactly what the problem was. Daniel had taken Sarah's side.

"Daniel is my husband. Of course I will do whatever he thinks is best," she finally said aloud.

Daniel's head jerked toward her, his smile entirely gone. "Oh, but—I did not mean—" he began.

But Miriam cut him off by getting to her feet. "Now then," she said briskly, "surely that is enough talk about the farm stand for one evening. I think it's high time we got these dishes done."

"Oh, don't bother about those," Amelia said as she got to her feet as well. Miriam kept her expression determined yet neutral as she looked into her mother-in-law's face. Was it her imagination, or did she see a certain compassion in Amelia's eyes?

"I am going to give you the same instructions I gave the young ones: It's a lovely evening. Go outside and enjoy yourselves. You'll have a fine night to walk home."

"No, Amelia," Miriam protested. "I can't walk away and leave you with so much work."

"Don't worry," Annaliese said. "I'll help."

"No, you won't," Amelia insisted. She put her hands on her hips. "Gracious, what's the matter with you all? Doing a few more dishes won't do me any harm." She extended her hands and regarded them thoughtfully. "Well, perhaps a few more wrinkles on my fingers." She gave a wry grin. "To match the ones around my eyes."

"Mamm," Daniel said. He got up from the table and bent to kiss his mother on the cheek. "You are generous, as always."

"Not to mention good-looking," Lucas said. He, too, got to his feet to give his mother a kiss. "Get Daed to help you," he said in a loud whisper. "He doesn't really do much of anything around this place."

"I heard that," Martin said.

"Thank you for the meal, Amelia," Sarah said. "I don't think there's a finer cook in all the district."

"Flattery will get you another invitation," Amelia said

with a smile. "Now, shoo, all of you! Let an old couple have some peace and quiet."

Daniel's father gave a snort. "I will see you tomorrow, then," he said.

"*Ja*, Daed," Daniel said as he held the door open for the others. "*Danki*. I appreciate the help."

"*We* appreciate the help," Miriam said. Then she stepped through the door. She paused for a moment, waiting for the others to join her. Amelia was right, she thought. It was a fine night. The fierce blue of the sky at midday had deepened to a lustrous indigo. The moon was up early, a glowing crescent of white in the sky.

"It's a firefly night," Annaliese said.

"*Ja!*" Miriam replied. "Though we do not see so many now."

"I will see you tomorrow," Lucas said.

Daniel nodded as he, Miriam, and Sarah turned in the direction of home. Just as they turned away, Miriam thought she saw Lucas reach for Annaliese's hand. Annaliese snatched it away, only to have Lucas reach for it again. From somewhere in the yard, Miriam heard happy shrieks and peals of laughter, Matthew chasing his sisters in some sort of game. She felt her heart swell with a bittersweet combination of joy and pain.

"Well, that was a lovely evening, don't you think?" Sarah asked as the three began to walk toward their house, Daniel in the middle with Miriam and Sarah on either side.

"*Ja,*" Miriam answered. "It is always a pleasure to go to Martin and Amelia's home."

"I'm glad you think so," Daniel answered, his tone just

as stilted and formal as Miriam's. "And I know Mamm appreciates the gift you brought. Was that the last of the blackberry jam?"

"*Ja,*" Miriam answered once more.

Sarah's gaze flickered between Daniel and Miriam as she spoke, as if she sensed that there was something wrong but wasn't quite certain of the cause.

"I'm sorry about the cell phone call," she suddenly burst out. "I know I should have mentioned that I had the phone with me. But it was just so lovely to see everyone that I forgot. It won't happen again, I—"

At just that moment, the phone went off once again.

"Oh, for pity's sake!" Sarah cried. She hung back, taking the phone out of her pocket. Miriam knew the second her sister answered the call. The shrill ring cut off.

"That's three calls from work today," Miriam said after a moment. "I hope that nothing is seriously wrong there."

"Sarah is very capable," Daniel said.

"*Ja,*" Miriam agreed. "She is."

"Then I'm sure she will sort things out."

They topped a small rise and now Miriam could see her own home below them. It looked quiet and peaceful in the still summer night, as if no turmoil could ever penetrate its sturdy walls. Sarah was still behind them, higher up on the hillside. The sound of her sister's voice floated down to Miriam, but she wasn't close enough to hear the words. Daniel moved forward and Miriam stepped quickly to catch up. Together they started down the last hill, toward home.

Did Lucas and Annaliese truly hold hands? Miriam wondered suddenly. Like a young, courting couple, not one who had been married for nearly five years and had a small child. Miriam cast a sidelong glance at Daniel. She could still just make out his features in the growing twilight. What would happen if she reached for his hand? Would she feel it curl around hers and hold as tight as it had when they were courting?

"Lucas told me a fine thing today," Daniel said as they walked along.

"Ach, ja?" Miriam said.

"They are going to have another *boppli*."

Miriam stumbled. Daniel reached quickly to steady her, his fingers closing around her upper arm.

"Oh, but that is wonderful news!" Miriam stammered, the truth of her words clear in the tone of her voice even as her heart bled a little at the news. "I wish them every joy. Are they hoping for a boy this time?"

"Probably," Daniel said. "I am glad to hear you are so happy for them," he said, his words all but tumbling over themselves, he spoke so quickly.

Miriam moved just as swiftly, stepping back, pulling out of Daniel's grasp. *"What?"*

"I only meant," Daniel began. He made as if to reach for her again, then stopped as Miriam took another step back. "It's just that I wondered how to tell you."

"You wondered how to tell me," Miriam echoed. "Why was that? Did you think I would not wish them joy? Do you really believe that I would be so selfish just because you and I—"

"Sorry, sorry!" Sarah's voice sliced across the conversation like a knife, and for once, Miriam was glad of the interruption. "No more tonight, I absolutely promise," Sarah went on as she came, panting, up to them. "I've turned the wretched thing off. Though, actually, they were calling with good news this time. A kid in our program who ran away from home last week has come back, thanks to God!"

Sarah's footsteps slowed, then stopped. In the dim light, Miriam saw her sister take in the space that separated Miriam and Daniel, the way they faced each other, like adversaries. Sarah's head swiveled between them as she tried to see the expressions their faces.

"What is it?" Sarah asked. "Is something wrong?"

"No." Miriam spoke up quickly and firmly, relieved that her voice did not falter, pleased that she had been quick to take control. "In fact, Daniel has some good news to share, but I will let him tell it. I am going to walk on ahead if you don't mind. There are some things I must do to be ready for tomorrow, and I'd like to get a head start on them. But you two take your time. Amelia is right. It's a lovely evening."

Without waiting for an answer, Miriam moved away from Daniel and turned toward home. She was still so close he could have stopped her with a touch, but Daniel did not reach out a second time. He simply stood, tall and silent as a fence post.

It was Sarah who protested her leaving. "Miriam," she said, "wait!"

But Miriam did not wait. She kept on going, her legs churning faster and faster as she moved downhill.

Don't run. Don't run. Don't run, she thought. Running would look, would *feel*, too much like running away. *And there's nowhere to run to,* she realized. There was only home. Home, without the father who had raised her, without the children Miriam longed to raise herself.

Miriam's body gave a great shudder and tears began to stream down her cheeks, hot enough to scald. Miriam had no idea when they had started. Now that they had, it seemed to her that they might never stop.

All that evening, she had been at cross-purposes with Daniel. They had been husband and wife for six years, and yet he didn't seem to understand the first thing about her. How was it possible that they shared the same bed and yet had become strangers to each other? Was this simply because Sarah was back, reminding Daniel of what he'd given up?

Miriam wiped her eyes with the back of her hand. Not so long ago, she would have said that Daniel was the center of her life. Daniel was where her heart found solace and joy. Now she had become so estranged from him, so lost, that Miriam wondered how she would ever find her way back again.

Seven

Leah's eyes flew wide open at first light. Had she slept at all? Sleep had seemed impossible when she'd gone to bed the night before. How could she sleep when there was so much to look forward to? Today was her first official day of work at the Stony Field Farm Stand. Leah didn't think she'd ever been more excited about anything in her whole life.

She tossed back the covers and rolled out of bed. She pulled up the bedclothes and then smoothed them so that they lay flat and tidy. She plumped up the pillow, then plopped it at the head of the bed. Leah had been performing this morning ritual for so long that she no longer even thought about it. It was simply what she did each and every morning.

In spite of her excitement, Leah paused to look down at her handiwork. She had made the summer quilt for her bed herself. It was a log cabin square, but the setting was called streak of lightning. The finished squares were arranged so that the sides with the same colors were adjacent to one another and formed diagonal zigzags from the top of the quilt to the bottom.

Like most quilts in Plain country, Leah's was made of solid colors. She had sewn the pink and green blocks together on Rachel's treadle sewing machine, but she had quilted the finished top by hand. The stitches were small and regular, evenly spaced, just the way quilting stitches should be. Aenti Rachel had praised the work, saying that Leah had a good hand with her needle and a good eye for color.

Someday I am going to make quilts to sell to Englischers, Leah thought. The *Englischers* loved the Plain quilts. If she could make quilts to sell, she could begin to contribute to her *aenti* and *onkel*'s household expenses. Or she could put some money away, getting ready for the day when she would have a household of her own. Perhaps if Miriam was satisfied with her work at the farm stand, Leah would be able to sell her quilts there.

You won't be able to sell a single thing if you're late your first morning, Leah, she thought. Filled with fresh purpose, Leah left her bedroom and marched downstairs to wash her hands and face for breakfast. Though she had absolutely no idea how she would manage to eat a single bite with all the butterflies dancing in her stomach.

* *

"*Ach*, Leah, *gut*, there you are," Miriam said. At the tone of Miriam's voice, Leah's already dancing stomach did a quick somersault. Miriam sounded so flustered!

"You know Victor King, don't you?" Miriam asked.

"*Ja*," Leah said, doing her best to hide her surprise. Of course she knew Victor King. He lived right down the road from her *aenti* and *onkel*. At the moment, he was sitting on the front seat of his farm wagon with a young man at his side. Leah snuck a quick glance at the back of the wagon. There was no produce to sell.

"*Gude mariye*, Victor," she said politely.

"*Gude mariye*, Leah," Victor responded pleasantly.

"And this is Victor's brother Eli," Miriam went on. "He's going to be working at the farm stand, too."

Leah bit down, hard, on the tip of her tongue. She was pretty sure it gave her face a pained expression, but it was better than the alternative: crying out that it wasn't fair. That working at the farm stand was supposed to be *her* special job.

"Oh, *ja*?" she said, her voice sounding foolish even to her own ears.

"*Ja*," Victor said shortly. He gave Eli a nudge. "Get down now, *kind*. I am late for the fields already. I'll come back at the end of the day."

At his brother's words, Eli's pale face flushed. *Mine would, too,* Leah thought in unexpected sympathy, *if somebody called me a child.* Why on earth hadn't Eli just walked to the farm stand? The King farm wasn't that far away.

Following his older brother's instructions, Eli swung down. As he stepped away from the wagon, moving toward Miriam and Leah, she could see that his gait was uneven. He pulled his right leg up short, as if putting his full weight on it was painful. That explained why he hadn't walked over, Leah thought, and most likely why he wasn't helping in the fields. But surely Eli could have borrowed Victor's wagon and driven himself to the farm stand. Why make his brother take time away from work at one of the busiest times of the year?

As soon as Eli was clear of the wagon, Victor clicked his tongue to the horse. It started forward. Victor gave one last wave to Miriam as the wagon pulled away from the farm stand and moved off down the road. Leah, Eli, and Miriam were left alone.

Leah couldn't help but look at Eli. He must have come to the district recently. She would definitely have remembered if she had seen him before. He had green eyes, pale skin, and a fringe of dark hair that she could just see poking out beneath the brim of his straw hat. Beneath the black suspenders, his shirt was a bright, crisp blue. It was so crisp she wondered if he was wearing it for the first time. He had a straight, wide mouth beneath high cheekbones, and, despite the limp, he stood tall and strong. What had she heard one of the older girls say about another boy? Eli was "good to look upon."

"Well, now, what shall we do first?" Miriam asked, her tone deliberately cheerful. "I know. Why don't the two of you bring the display tables out front? That is, if you think that you can manage, Eli. I can see that leg still bothers you."

"I can manage," Eli answered shortly.

"Fine," Miriam said. "Bring out the tables, then, you two. That way, we'll be all ready when our neighbors arrive."

"How did you hurt your leg?" Leah asked some time later. The last half hour or so had been busy with people arriving with produce to sell. Miriam had kept Leah and Eli working together, arranging the fruits and vegetables on the outside display tables. For the most part, they had worked in silence. It was beginning to get on Leah's nerves.

Eli cast her a sidelong glance, a definite challenge in his eyes. Eli's eyes were the greenest that Leah had ever seen. They stood out in vivid contrast to his pale skin and dark hair. They would have been beautiful if they weren't so cold, she thought.

"As if you don't already know," he said now.

Leah gasped. In the first place, he sounded so *Englisch*! In the second place, he was so wrong! And in the third . . . did he really have to be so rude? All Leah was doing was trying to make conversation.

"Why would I ask if I already knew the answer?" she demanded.

Eli gave a snort. "How should I know?"

All of a sudden, Leah's irritation vanished. The laugh bubbled up and out of her before she could call it back.

At the sound of it, Eli's face flushed. "You think this is funny?"

Leah sighed. "Of course I think it's funny," she said. "Can you really not hear how ridiculous we sound? All this

103

knowing and not knowing. But I do not think it's funny that you are hurt. That isn't what I meant at all. How it happened is none of my business. I won't ask again, and I am sorry to have intruded on your privacy."

There! That ought to put rude Eli King in his place! she thought.

Eli stared then reached into a crate of tomatoes and began arranging them in neat rows. "Do you always talk like that?" he asked after a moment.

"Like what?"

"Like you're already a *gross-mammi*."

"I do not sound like a grandmother!" Leah protested, all her irritation returning. "I was just trying to be polite."

"Well, don't be," Eli said. "In my experience, people use politeness as an excuse to hide what they really mean. Usually, it's something not very nice. I'd rather just know what people think, right out."

"All right," Leah replied. She put her hands on her hips, just like her *aenti* Rachel did when she got cross. "What I *think*, Eli, is that you don't understand the first thing about what it really means to be polite. What I *think* is that you're rude and inconsiderate, and I feel sorry for you. What I *think* is that this conversation is over. I'm going to ask Miriam for something else to do, and though I won't request it of her, hopefully she will give me something where I won't have to get a lesson from you."

"Where do you think we should put the pickles?" Leah asked Eli. Though she had hoped for a new assignment, far from his moody self, Miriam had directed them both to unpack and display the huge carton of condiments that Mary Helmuth had delivered that morning.

Leah had carefully lined up jars of chow-chow, horse-radish, and chutneys on one of the stand's side shelves. Now she was out of room.

Eli didn't even look at her. He just shrugged and said, "How about near the register? The farm stands where I come from, in Ohio, always put the pickles near the register."

"It's already crowded there with jams and jellies," Leah said, dismissing the idea.

"Then find another place for them," Eli told her.

Twenty minutes later, Leah still had a half dozen pickle jars and no place to put them. Eli, she noticed, had found places for the mustards and relishes that he was unpacking.

"Pickles!" she said, exasperated.

Instantly, she became the focus of three pairs of eyes: Miriam's, Sarah's, and Eli's. Miriam's looked puzzled, Sarah's intrigued. And, as Leah was beginning to suspect might always be the case, it was impossible to read the expression in Eli's.

"Pickles?" Sarah echoed.

Leah glanced around in desperation. She had to figure out something now. She was not going to have Miriam think that it was taking her an entire day to find a home for these infernal pickles.

Leah gestured to the display of preserves and canned goods that now sat prominently on the farm stand's front counter.

"It needs some pickles," she explained. She marched

over to the counter, nudged a few of the jams and jellies to the side, and wedged two jars of pickles beside the register. Surprisingly, they didn't look out of place. "This way customers can't possibly miss them as they check out. Everything we have out now is sweet," Leah went on. "But not everybody wants that, at least not all the time."

"It's not a bad idea," Sarah said thoughtfully.

"It was Eli's," Leah admitted. She couldn't rightfully take credit for something he had thought of.

Eli murmured something Leah couldn't quite catch beneath his breath. She ignored him.

"We need a variety, don't you think?" she said, appealing to Sarah.

"A variety." Sarah pronounced the words as if absolutely delighted by them. "Leah, you are absolutely right." Her bright blue eyes, so much like her older sister's, traveled between Leah and Eli. "I don't know what you think, Miriam, but I'd say these two make a pretty good team."

"Working together is always a blessing," Miriam replied, somewhat neutrally. "There are more pickles on the shelves at the back of the store, different types." She smiled at Leah. "But then, you know that, Leah, from helping me yesterday. I will let you and Eli decide which ones we should have on display." She shot Sarah a quick look. "Since you make such a good team. You'll probably need the stepladder," she added.

Then she moved away from the counter to help a customer outside, with Sarah trailing along behind. Leah and Eli were left alone.

"I can't climb the ladder. My leg is too stiff," Eli said at once.

Leah's stomach did a quick dive. She was secretly afraid of even the smallest height. Not that she was about to admit that to Eli, of course. Instead, she gave her head a toss, sending the strings of her *kapp* flying.

"I know how to climb a ladder," she said.

"Fine," Eli answered shortly. "Then you won't mind if I help out front." He gestured toward the outside. "Looks like we're busy all of a sudden."

Gazing out the open doors of the farm stand, Leah could see that he was right. Miriam and Sarah were each helping *Englisch* customers, and there were more cars just pulling into the parking lot.

"Fine," Leah said, echoing Eli's word.

Without waiting for him to make the first move, she spun on one heel and marched toward the back of the farm stand, heading for the place where the stepladder was stored behind the open back door. It was taller than the one her *aenti* Rachel used to reach high shelves in the kitchen, a half dozen steps up instead of just two. But, like Aenti Rachel's, it had a curved bar at the top to hang on to, and a shelf just below that. Though Onkel John insisted it was there to be used, Aenti Rachel had always been dead set against putting anything on that shelf.

Leah hefted the stepladder—it was heavier than the one at home, too—and then walked to the shelves at the very back of the stand. To reach the pickles, she would have to climb at least three steps. Just the thought made her hands cold and clammy.

Don't you be a child, now, Leah, she thought.

She set the ladder down and opened it up just as a peal

of childish laughter filtered in from out of doors. Leah snuck a quick glance over her shoulder. Eli was helping an *Englisch* family with several young children. As she watched, he reached down and swung a young boy up onto his shoulders.

Well, Leah thought, *at least he can be nice to someone!*

She turned back to the ladder, pulled in a deep breath, and began to climb. She moved quickly, as if afraid to lose momentum, and kept her eyes fixed straight ahead, on the items on the shelves. As soon as the first jars of pickles came into view in front of her, Leah stopped. Then she reached out and seized several tall jars of dill pickle spears. After a moment's hesitation, she placed them on the step-ladder shelf.

Aenti Rachel would *definitely* not approve. But Leah did not want to go up and down the ladder umpteen times. Once up and once down was bad enough. Go up, collect the pickle jars she needed, come back down.

Leah stared at the shelves. She really should have some bread and butter pickles, too, she decided. After all, she had been the one to use the word "variety." Fortunately, the jars of the thin, flat pickle slices were small. Unfortunately, they were on the next-to-the-highest shelf.

Leah's heart began to race. Her legs and feet felt as if they were made of lead. She gritted her teeth and climbed one step higher, and then another. One more step, and she'd be on the top step. And here, finally, her *aenti* Rachel's opinion won out. Aenti Rachel would *never* approve of standing on the top step.

Leah arched onto her tiptoes, reaching for the pickles.

Her fingers found the first jar. It scooted backward, out of reach. She shifted position, trying to stretch up as high as she could. Her efforts made the ladder rock ever so slightly. One of the jars of dill pickles on the ladder shelf began to tilt.

Oh, no! Leah's heart leapt into her throat. Desperately, she abandoned her quest for the sweet pickles and came down a step, making a lunge for the jar that was about to fall. The ladder swayed even more. Leah caught up all the jars she had pulled from the shelves, clutching them to her chest, and felt the ladder begin to rock in the opposite direction. She was going to fall!

Utterly without warning, Leah felt a pair of strong arms wrap around her, plucking her from the ladder and spinning her around. She was back on her feet almost before she realized what was happening. She stood, slightly breathless, still clutching the jars of pickles to her chest, and stared up into the face of her rescuer.

It was Eli.

Eli's face was flushed. His chest rose and fell quickly. He was breathing hard, as if he had just sprinted to reach the back of the farm stand. His green eyes were wide and startled as they gazed down into Leah's.

How had she ever thought his eyes were cold? Up close, they were anything but. Up close, Eli's green eyes seemed lit from within, burning with some secret inner fire. Leah swayed, her head dropping forward as if she longed to rest it on his shoulder. She could have sworn she felt Eli's arms tighten.

"First time on a ladder?" he inquired.

Leah's head jerked up. She yanked back, out of Eli's arms. She could feel her face grow hot with humiliation. Eli made a gesture, as if to call her back. Leah took a second step back and bumped right into the stepladder.

Why, oh, why couldn't she think of some scathing reply? More than anything in the world, what Leah wanted was to hear her own voice delivering some finely chosen words. Words that would put Eli in his place once and for all. Preferably a place that was far away from Leah. But Leah's mind was as blank as a new piece of paper. Her throat felt thick, as if she were about to cry.

She sidled sideways, still carrying her precious load of pickles, until she was certain she was out of the reach of Eli's long arms. Then she whirled and walked to the front of the farm stand as quickly as she could, desperately trying to ignore the way her legs threatened to wobble.

"*Danki*, Leah," Miriam said as she came in from outside. "Those will be a great addition to the display. You were right."

Leah swallowed hard. "I was thinking some bread and butter pickles, too," she admitted, "but I—"

"Oh," Miriam said as her gaze slid past Leah. "Thank you, Eli."

Out of the corner of her eye, Leah saw several jars of bread and butter pickles materialize on the counter near the display. She did not turn her head, but she did find her voice.

"Yes, thank you, Eli."

"I think we've done enough for today," Miriam went on. If she noticed any tension between the two young people, Leah could not tell. "We can put the finishing touches on the display tomorrow morning. Good work today, both of you. Thank you very much. Sarah and I can close up the stand. You can go on home now."

"I will stay and help you," Eli said. "I must wait for my *onkel*. The doctor in Ohio said I must not walk too far."

"All right, then," Miriam said. "See you tomorrow, Leah."

"See you tomorrow," Leah said.

She walked out the big front doors of the farm stand without looking back. If she looked back, she would have to look at Eli.

Quickly, with determined steps, Leah crossed the road and headed for home. What had happened in those moments after Eli had saved her from what could have been a nasty fall? Did she even really want to know?

No, she decided, as she turned down the driveway to her *aenti* and *onkel*'s house. She did not. She didn't want to get any closer to the surprising glimpse of fire in Eli King's cool, green eyes. Because one thing about fire, if you got close enough, you got burned. Every single time.

Eight

It was amazing how quickly new situations became old ones, Miriam thought. She stood, hands on hips, in the late morning sunshine, gazing at the farm stand from across the road. Was it really just a few short weeks ago that she had wondered how she would ever keep the stand running? God had certainly answered that question, and in a way Miriam would never have anticipated: by providing both Leah and Eli.

But that was the thing about God's work, Miriam thought. You could always trust that He would act, but you couldn't always see the ways of it ahead of time.

Take what she was doing now, for instance. Looking at a place she knew both inside and out from a distance rather than the usual up close. It was giving Miriam a whole new perspective on the farm stand, one she was finding both useful and inspiring. But the simple act of crossing the road to see the stand might never have occurred to her if not for an offhand remark of Leah's about how she always looked forward to the moment the farm stand first came into view as she approached it from her *aenti* and *onkel*'s home.

It made Miriam realize how much she, too, looked forward to her first glimpse of the farm stand each and every day. But it also made her realize that she saw the same thing, time after time. Leah's remark had inspired her to take a moment each day to look at the farm stand from a different angle. Sarah teased her about it, claiming that it looked as if Miriam were looking for the missing piece to a puzzle.

It was more than that, Miriam knew. Secretly, she suspected that what she was really looking for was the puzzle itself. If she ever had all the pieces, she might see a way into Daniel's heart.

And that's enough searching for today, she decided. She would be late to start Daniel's midday dinner if she didn't get a move on. Moving briskly, Miriam walked back across the road.

"I think the farm stand could use a new coat of paint after we close for the winter," Miriam said at dinner.

"Oh, *ja*?" Daniel asked somewhat absently. He turned the page of the farm journal he was reading and did not look up.

"Ja," Miriam replied.

Quickly, she cut a piece from a slice of ripe tomato and popped it in her mouth. As far as Miriam was concerned, tomatoes were the true taste of summer. But that wasn't the reason she was so eager to eat one now. She was trying to fill her mouth with something other than tart words. For once, Miriam had Daniel all to herself. Sarah had gone to run a quick errand in town, and Leah and Eli were minding the farm stand alone for the time being. Miriam would take dinner down to them once she and Daniel were finished eating.

Miriam had been secretly tickled to think she and Daniel would actually have a meal alone. And what was he doing? Reading a farm journal. Miriam knew that reading the journal was important to Daniel. But did he have to do it *now*?

She swallowed. "I am thinking we might make a change," she continued. "Something that customers could see from far away. What would you think of painting the sides of the stand orange with red stripes?"

"That sounds nice," Daniel commented. He turned another page of the journal and continued reading. Then, all of a sudden, he paused. He looked up, eyebrows raised, forehead creased in confusion. "Wait. What did you say?"

"Never mind," Miriam said. She stood up. She picked up her plate and gave it a quick dunk in the dishwater she had ready and waiting in the sink. Then she rinsed it and set it in the drainer to dry. "I should get back. The young ones are on their own. I will see you at supper tonight, Daniel."

"Miriam," Daniel said. "I . . ."

But Miriam was in no mood to wait. Thrusting her feet

into her waiting clogs, she snatched up the meals she had prepared for Leah and Eli, gave the kitchen screen door a shove, and stepped out onto the porch. And then she was moving swiftly away from the house, the taste of the words she had tried so hard not to say leaving a strange, bitter flavor in her mouth as the screen door banged shut behind her.

Wham!

A car door slammed and Leah whirled toward the sound. She was just in time to see an *Englisch* guy not much older than she was come around the side of a bright red car. The car was sleek and lean and so low, it seemed to hug the ground. In the weeks since she had started working at the farm stand, Leah had seen more kinds of cars than she'd ever known existed. But she had never seen a car like this before.

The passenger door opened and a second young man got out. Like the first, he wore dark jeans. But where the driver wore a pristine white T-shirt, the guy in the passenger seat wore no shirt at all! Quickly, Leah lowered her eyes.

I can handle this, she thought. Besides, it wasn't as if she had much choice. Sarah had left to run an errand, and Eli wasn't anywhere in sight.

"I'm sorry about my friend," Leah heard a deep voice say.

She raised her eyes, focusing on his face. The driver was tall. So tall that Leah had to tilt her head back to see him clearly. *How on earth does he fit his legs into that tiny car?* she wondered. The young *Englischer*'s face was very tan.

"He doesn't mean any harm," the young man went on. He flashed Leah an easy smile, revealing a set of perfectly even white teeth. "He just always wants pretty girls to notice him, that's all."

Leah was glad her own smile was already in place. It was something Sarah had taught her. Always smile at an approaching customer. But still, she felt her cheeks begin to grow hot. She was blushing, and, even worse, Leah was pretty sure this particular customer would misunderstand the cause.

Does he think I'm stupid? she wondered. *Just because I'm Plain.* Or maybe *Englisch* girls liked that sort of remark. In which case, Leah was glad she wasn't one of them.

"May I help you?" she asked politely.

"Oh, I think so," the young man said. "I'm looking for something . . . very special."

"Is it for a special occasion?" Leah asked, feeling a little better now that she had found a way to deflect his remark. Asking this question was also something she had learned from Sarah.

"Yes," the young *Englischer* said at once. "I, uh, need to make a good first impression."

"Oh, well, in that case," Leah said, "I'm sure I can help."

She turned away from him and walked around to the far side of the display table, so that she would be better able to point out some selections. Leah was feeling much more comfortable now. She was pretty sure this young man had

117

just lied to her. That made helping him easier, in a way. In the time she had worked at the farm stand, Leah had encountered this kind of *Englischer* before. He *did* think she was stupid because she wasn't like him. So stupid that she would be blinded by idle compliments and the sight of a fancy red car.

"These berries are very nice," she said, gesturing to the basket she had set out just moments before. "And very fresh. They were picked just this morning."

"Hey, Steve," called out his passenger, who was leaning against the car. "We haven't got all day. Come on."

"In a minute," the guy named Steve yelled back without turning around. "Keep your shirt on."

The guy at the car gave a snort of laughter. Leah didn't let her eyes so much as flicker in his direction, but an idea was beginning to take shape in the back of her mind.

"So this is the best you've got," Steve said.

"Oh, no," Leah answered with a smile. "Everything here is good. May I show you something else?"

Steve hesitated for a second, and then seemed to make up his mind. "No, that's okay," he said. "On second thought, I'm not so sure you have anything I want after all."

"I'm sorry to hear you say that," Leah said. She picked up the basket of berries quickly, before she could change her mind. Then she walked around the end of the table, making straight for the guy leaning against the car. He straightened up at her approach.

"These are for you," Leah said. She held the basket out and gave him her very best smile. He took them, the startled expression on his face betraying his surprise. Leah turned back toward Steve. "It was so nice of you both to stop by. We get new produce all the time, so come back anytime."

Her back as straight as one of Aenti Rachel's dining room chairs, Leah turned and walked toward the farm stand. She didn't stop until she was all the way inside.

I did it! she thought. She had showed those *Englisch* boys! She hadn't let them make fun of her. She'd stood up for herself. Leah stepped behind the counter, turning just as she heard the car's engine spring to life. It backed up quickly, spraying gravel. Then, with a squeal of tires, it roared off down the road.

"What do you think you're doing?" an angry voice demanded.

Startled, Leah swung around. Eli was standing just behind her. In her eagerness to reach the safety of the inside of the building, Leah hadn't noticed him.

"Waiting on a customer. What does it look like I'm doing?" she snapped.

"Honestly?" Eli asked, his tone challenging.

And I'm not afraid of you, either, Eli King, Leah thought. She lifted her chin, meeting his green eyes squarely.

"Yes, honestly."

"It looks like you're flirting with *Englisch* boys."

Leah gasped. The way the *Englisch* boy had treated her had made her angry, but it was nothing compared to this.

"I don't care what it looks like."

"Well, you ought to," Eli replied. "You don't want to get a reputation."

"A *reputation*!" Leah cried. "Now who's sounding like

119

a *gross-mammi*? You are not in charge of me, Eli King, so stop acting like you are. Stop acting like you know me when you don't. You don't know me at all."

"Forget it," Eli said in a tight, cold voice. "You don't want to listen, fine. But don't come crying to me when you find out everybody's been talking behind your back. Don't come crying to me when something goes wrong."

"You bet I won't," Leah said. "You're the last person on earth I'd turn to. And nothing's going to *go wrong*."

"Gracious, you two!" Miriam's voice sliced across the argument. "I could hear you halfway down the drive from the house. What is the matter here?"

"Nothing," Leah answered shortly. She met Eli's eyes, daring him to contradict her. "Eli and I were just having a difference of opinion, that's all. A small one."

"Eli?" Miriam queried.

"It is as Leah says," Eli replied. "We had a difference of opinion, but I think we both know where we stand now."

We do indeed, Leah thought. *As far away from each other as possible!*

Where is everybody? Miriam wondered.

It was a hot, sticky evening in late July, and she stood at the kitchen counter, surveying the stack of supper dishes. Usually Sarah offered to help with the washing up, although Miriam steadfastly refused. She was unwilling to let Sarah help with any of the tasks that rightfully belonged to her, as Daniel's wife. Tonight, however, not only had Sarah not offered, she was nowhere to be found!

I suppose this is what I get for always refusing her help, Miriam thought a little wryly as she moved to the sink. She turned on the hot water to fill the basin and heard a quick peal of laughter from outside.

That's Sarah's voice, she thought. She glanced out the kitchen window, but the stretch of yard that she could see through the window was empty. Acting on impulse, Miriam shut off the water and headed for the living room. She pushed the screen door open and looked out. Sarah was nowhere in sight. But once again, Miriam heard the sound of her sister's laughter, high and joyful and bright.

That's coming from the direction of the barn, she thought. She stepped outside, moving in the direction of the sound. She had just rounded the corner of the house when she saw Sarah and Daniel coming toward the house.

They had their arms around each other.

Miriam's heart began to thunder in her chest. Desperately, she tried to make sense of what was right before her eyes. Sarah had one shoe off. One of those ridiculous platform sandals that had garnered so much attention the first time she'd worn them. Miriam could see it, dangling from her sister's outstretched fingers. The shoe was covered in muck. But with her other hand, Sarah was holding on to Daniel for support, one arm looped around his neck. Daniel had a supporting arm around Sarah's waist. Their bodies were close together, bumping together every time they took a step.

"Daniel," Sarah protested, and even from a distance Miriam could hear the laughter in her sister's voice. "You're going too fast. Slow down!"

"It's you who should hurry up," Daniel replied, his tone both amused and exasperated. "The sooner we get back to the house, the sooner you can get cleaned up. Though I do not understand why you want to wear such ridiculous footwear in the first place."

"Because . . ." Sarah began.

She waved the shoe she was carrying for emphasis. Muck from the bottom of the shoe went flying. Daniel jerked back, threatening to tug them both off balance. Sarah tightened her hold, pulling him back toward her even as she laughed once more. And suddenly, incredibly, Daniel began to laugh as well. Miriam's quiet and reserved husband was walking across their yard with his arm around her sister, laughing.

Like a love-struck schoolboy, Miriam thought. Pain, clean and swift as the stroke of a knife, sliced through Miriam's heart.

"Oh, Miriam." As if from a great distance, Miriam heard her sister's voice. At the sound of Miriam's name, Daniel's head swiveled in her direction. His arm dropped away from Sarah. He took a single step back and, this time, Sarah released her hold. She and Daniel were separate once more. But Miriam knew that she would see the image from this evening forever. It had been burned into her mind, into her heart. And at that moment, Miriam was seized by a desire so powerful her body quivered with it.

I must not let them know.

Neither Daniel nor Sarah must ever know the pain this moment had brought to Miriam, this moment that was the living confirmation of all her fears and the death of all her hopes. She had kept her fears a secret, kept them to herself for all these years. Surely she was strong enough to keep them locked inside her now.

She smiled.

"Looks like you're having some trouble," she said. And at the sound of her own voice, so bright and natural, Miriam felt a quick surge of relief. She clung to it, the life raft that would save her from slipping beneath the deep water of her pain.

"I know. Can you believe it?" Sarah said, precisely as if there was nothing wrong at all. Nothing unusual about walking across the yard with her arms around her sister's husband. "I went out to the barn to see the horses and I just wasn't thinking and I . . ." She made as if to wave the shoe once more.

"Sarah," Daniel said in a low voice.

Sarah turned to look at Daniel. For the first time, she seemed to realize that he was no longer right by her side. She took in his sober, almost frowning expression.

"What?" she said. Her glance went from Miriam to Daniel and back again, as if finally taking in the fact that Miriam was smiling but Daniel was not. "What's happened?" she asked. "Is something wrong?"

"Of course not," Miriam answered quickly. Too quickly, she thought. But suddenly it seemed to her she could not bear to hear what Daniel would answer. Could not bear to know whether or not he *could* answer. Did he, too, think that there was nothing wrong? Nothing wrong with walking across the yard with his arms around Sarah when the only time he touched Miriam was in their bedroom at night.

"I came out because I thought I heard a mockingbird singing," Miriam lied. But she had always loved mockingbirds, and both her husband and her sister knew that. Now she wondered if it was because the mockingbird was so skilled at disguising its true nature, a skill *she* was becoming quite practiced at. Miriam had never thought of herself as a dishonest person, but here she was, lying to two of the people she loved best.

She tilted her head toward the house. "I'd better get back and get the supper dishes taken care of. I can bring you some rags for those shoes, if you like."

"That's all right," Sarah said. "It's my mess. I can clean it up myself. After that, I'll come help with the washing up."

No! Miriam wanted to cry out. It seemed to her that her whole body ached suddenly with the need to shout. To tell Sarah, once and for all, that she did not need her help. Miriam might have lost Daniel, but she still had this much. She could care for her own home.

And still Daniel said nothing. *Did* nothing. No. That was not quite right, Miriam thought. He had taken Sarah's arm. He had spoken Sarah's name. Sarah's, not Miriam's. He had not spoken the name of his wife. He had taken a step away from Sarah, but not one single step toward Miriam. Instead, Daniel had simply continued to stand, arms hanging loosely by his sides, in the middle of the yard.

"You don't have to do that," she said with a brittle laugh, so different from Sarah's open and spontaneous one. "I can manage on my own. You should stay outdoors. It really is a lovely night. There won't be many like this while you're here."

And soon, Miriam thought as she turned away, *soon you will be gone. Back to San Francisco. Back where you belong.*

What life would be like then, Miriam simply could not bear to contemplate. Her back ramrod straight, she crossed the yard and went back inside the house.

Nine

The days that followed were some of the most beautiful Miriam could ever remember. Summer was in full swing now with July rolling to a close. The days were lush and warm. Miriam could see summer's promise being fulfilled in every direction. Corn stood high in the fields, the tall green stalks swaying with the breeze, their tasseled heads glinting in the sunshine. New-mown hay ripened in fat, round rolls. The rosebushes Miriam grew for the hips they would create in the autumn were a fluttering mass of pink and white blossoms as they formed one long border of her kitchen garden. The scent of the flowers was so potent, Miriam could smell it even when she was indoors.

And as for the farm stand, it bustled. That was really the only way to describe it, Miriam thought as she threw open the front doors. She had walked down to the stand earlier than usual this morning, eager to have a few moments alone. Were there more tourists than usual on the road this year? Were the harvests particularly fine so that everyone had more to bring her than usual? Or were her friends and neighbors taking extra care to support the Stony Field Farm Stand now that Miriam's father was gone? Miriam genuinely did not know. All she knew was that, between running the farm stand and running the house, Miriam was busy from morning 'til night.

She had never in her life been so grateful for hard work. There were days when it seemed to Miriam that the tasks that made up her day-to-day life were the only things she truly understood anymore. The only moments when she felt she knew the way the world worked, when she could clearly see her own place in it, when she understood who she herself was.

Miriam knew how to iron her *kapps* so that the pleats stayed stiff and neat. She knew just how long the bread should rise. She knew so many different ways to put up fruits, vegetables, and meats that she had long since ceased to count them all. In the days that had followed the encounter with Sarah and Daniel in the yard outside the barn, Miriam immersed herself in the day-to-day tasks that kept her so busy. She had always found pleasure in even the simplest of them, but now it seemed to her that those tasks kept her safe as well.

They were her protection against the pain that seemed to dog her every step, overtaking her the moment she stopped moving, snatching at whatever peace of mind she had won.

Her chores were her shield against the dizziness that would appear from out of nowhere, so sudden and powerful that Miriam would have to stop whatever she was doing and sit down.

Never had she felt as alone as she did in those moments, so weak, so unlike herself. The space between her and Daniel yawned in front of her, so wide and deep that it seemed to Miriam that she could no longer see Daniel across it. Those moments were the very worst of all. For in them, Miriam felt a new fear, one that seemed determined to break her already fractured heart: that the time for understanding between her and Daniel was gone forever. It was irretrievably lost.

Sometimes, in the evenings, Miriam would lift her head from whatever she was doing to find Daniel's gaze upon her, his expression unreadable. But even in the moments they had alone—at the breakfast table in the early morning, in their room at night—not once had Daniel spoken. Did this mean that he had nothing to say to her? Miriam wondered. Or was it just the opposite? Did he want to say too much?

And always, always, there was Sarah. Even when she wasn't in the room, it seemed to Miriam that her sister was present, hovering like a shadow at Daniel's side. Though Sarah spending time with Daniel was hardly a trick of Miriam's imagination. She saw them together often enough. There were days when it seemed to Miriam that she saw Sarah and Daniel together every time she turned around.

She would look up from preparing dinner to see Sarah and Daniel coming across the fields together, as if Sarah had finished up her own work at the farm stand and then gone to meet Daniel for the express purpose of walking him home. In the evenings after supper, they often worked a jigsaw puzzle, their heads close together as they bent to study the shapes of the pieces. One night, Daniel fetched a pencil and paper, and he and Sarah worked all evening on a design for an arbor she was hoping her young gardeners might build after her return to San Francisco.

There was only one place where Miriam was certain she would never find Sarah, and that was the bedroom Miriam and Daniel shared. But Miriam feared bringing up the topic of Daniel's feelings for her sister in this room. She feared it with every fiber of her being. The kitchen might be the heart of the house, but the room shared by a husband and wife provided its lifeblood. For it was here that a wife and husband were most intimate, where they shared things between themselves alone. In this room, future generations would be created.

But the moment Miriam spoke Sarah's name aloud in that special place, Miriam and Daniel would no longer be alone. Sarah would be with them, even there, leaving Miriam with no place left in all the world where she could have Daniel all to herself.

The possibility that her fears were the truth—and Daniel really did love Sarah—was like a mirror held up to the sun, too painfully bright for Miriam to look upon.

"Miriam?"

At the sound of her own name, Miriam jumped and spun around. Leah stood hesitating just inside the open doors of the farm stand, balanced on the balls of her feet, as if uncertain whether to step forward or back.

"Oh, I'm so sorry," she went on at once. "I didn't mean to startle you."

"It is my fault," Miriam said. "I got lost in my own thoughts. But you're here so early, Leah. Has something happened? Is something wrong?"

"Oh, Miriam," Leah sobbed out.

Miriam forgot her own problems in an instant. Quickly, she hurried to the younger woman's side.

"Gracious, Leah, what is it?" she asked. She put her hands on Leah's shoulders and peered down into her face. It was clear that Leah was, and had been, crying. "Has there been an accident? Is Rachel or John unwell?"

"No, no, it's nothing like that," Leah said. She scrubbed at her damp cheeks with impatient fingers. "It may sound foolish, but . . . I broke a lamp while I was dusting this morning. I was thinking about something else and I . . ." She choked back another sob. "Aenti Rachel would never say it is her favorite, but I know she treasured it. She has had it since she married Onkel John. I would like to go into town to replace it, though I know whatever I find won't be the same. And you probably think I'm silly for making such a fuss over just a lamp."

"Of course I don't think that," Miriam said. "And of course you must go at once. We're never very busy first thing in the morning, and the stores should be open by the time you get to town. Take your time, Leah. Make sure you are thoughtful in what you decide. That will make your aunt feel better."

Leah gave a shaky laugh. "*Danki*, Miriam. You really do sound just like her sometimes."

Miriam gave Leah a quick hug, and then let her go. "Off with you, now. Stop and show me what you picked out before you go home."

"I will," Leah promised.

She turned and dashed back across the road, sprinting for home. Miriam turned back to the farm stand with a smile. There was nothing like somebody else's troubles to help you forget your own, she thought, even when those troubles were small. Though they hadn't seemed small to Leah!

It was time to get out the tables and ready the farm stand for the day, and unless Eli or Sarah showed up soon, it looked as if Miriam would be performing that task herself.

She went back inside, determined to get the display tables out front without dropping anything on her foot this time.

"Oh, *thank you*, Mr. Wilson," Leah breathed. "You are right. That is the perfect one. It's almost like the old one, isn't it?"

"Pretty close," Angus Wilson said. He owned the hardware store in town. It was one of the biggest stores on the main street, catering to both Amish and *Englisch* customers. "Do you know, I actually remember that lamp you're talking about? It was one of the most popular styles, for quite a while."

"Why would they change it if everybody liked it so much?" Leah asked.

Angus Wilson smiled. "That's a very good question, young lady," he said. "And I'm sorry to say it's one I don't have a good answer for. Now, you wait right there and I'll go get one that's all boxed up for you."

"*Danki*, Mr. Wilson," Leah said.

While she waited, she strolled around a bit. Leah loved the hardware store. Loved the way the things that pretty much only Plain folk would use sat right next to the things the *Englisch* preferred. And then there were the things that suited both equally well. She paused in front of one of the big storefront windows, admiring the display. Across the street, she saw a young Plain man come out of Tompkins Lumber. He set off down the street, his gait a little slow and halting.

But surely that is Eli! Leah thought.

She shifted position, angling for a better view. *Ja*, it was definitely Eli. What on earth was he doing in town when he was supposed to be at the farm stand? Miriam hadn't said anything about Eli also coming into town. He turned the corner and Leah lost sight of him.

"Here we go, Leah." Mr. Wilson's voice sounded behind her. "All boxed up safe and sound. You be sure to give your aunt and uncle my best."

"I will, Mr. Wilson," Leah promised as she turned away from the window. "Thank you again for all your help."

The new lamp safely in hand, Leah left the store. She looked up ahead to try to see Eli, but there was no sign of him. *I shouldn't care,* Leah thought to herself—but what was Eli doing in town? What was he up to?

* *

The road from town was long and straight, an easy ride punctuated by gentle hills and stretches of flat land. Leah had always enjoyed the route between town and her *aenti* and *onkel*'s home. The sound of the horse's hooves was brisk and cheerful against the hard surface of the roadway. At this time of day, still fairly early, there were mostly farm vehicles, with Plain folk running errands or going to their fields. Tractors, buggies, and farm vehicles drawn by horses and mules traveled along the road in a stream of slow-moving but steady traffic.

Leah had just passed the silo that marked the end of the outskirts of town and the start of open country when she saw a figure walking by the side of the road. Even if she hadn't seen him leaving Tompkins Lumber Supply, Leah would have known that it was Eli. The walker's gait was ever so slightly uneven, favoring the right leg.

Why hadn't he driven to town? Leah wondered.

Eli's leg was much better, so much so that Victor no longer drove his younger brother to work at the farm stand. But as far as she could remember, Leah didn't think she had ever seen Eli drive. She pulled back gently on the reins, slowing the buggy to a walk. Eli turned.

"Would you like a ride?" Leah offered.

Eli hesitated and, for a split second, Leah thought he would decline. Then he gave a quick nod.

"Danki," he said.

Leah guided the buggy onto the shoulder of the road and

stopped. Eli swung up and settled in beside her. Leah looked back over her shoulder to make sure the way was clear. Then she chirruped to the horse and pulled back onto the road. She and Eli drove in silence for several moments. Leah wanted to ask him why he was in town, but she didn't want to appear to be all that interested. After a few more minutes, Leah was wondering if Eli intended to remain silent all the way back to the farm stand. But then he spoke.

"*Danki,*" he said once more. "It is very nice of you to stop for me."

"Some people think I'm very nice," Leah commented. She kept her eyes straight ahead, looking between the horse's ears at the stretch of road directly in front of her.

"Do they?" Eli inquired.

"Oh, *ja,* they do," Leah said. "I could draw up a list, if you like."

"I don't think that will be necessary," Eli said pleasantly. "I trust you."

"Do you, now?"

Before Eli could answer, Leah clicked her tongue to the horse, encouraging the mare to pick up her pace as they climbed a small hill. As they came back down, she shot a quick glance at him out of the corner of her eye.

"Would you like to know something?" he asked.

"If you would like to tell me."

"The answer to your question is yes. I believe I do trust you."

"I can't think why," Leah commented. "Most of the time, we don't even like each other very much."

"To tell you the truth, neither can I."

All of a sudden, Leah laughed. A fraction of a second later, Eli laughed, too, the sound full-throated and surprised.

"Thank goodness we got *that* straightened out," Leah said. She guided the horse down another hill.

"Leah, I have a proposal for you," Eli said.

"What?"

"I'd like to propose a truce," he went on. "I think that we got off on the wrong foot, you and I. Do you think we could start over?"

"No," Leah said. She shot a glance in Eli's direction just in time to see a dark blush suffuse his face. "But I think that we could start fresh, from right now. My *onkel* John says you can never start over, but it is never too late to start walking with God."

"I should have known you'd have something like that to say," Eli remarked, but there was no sting in his tone. He held out a hand. "Truce?"

Leah relinquished her grip on the reins long enough to put one hand in Eli's. "Truce."

They shook hands, then drove in silence for several moments.

"Do you like living with Victor?" Leah finally inquired.

"Ja," Eli answered shortly, and Leah thought he sounded surprised by his own reply. "I wasn't certain I would, at first. He is very strict, but now that I have been with him a while . . . he's fair, too. That's more important, I think."

"I think so, too."

"Watch out," Eli said with a sudden grin. "We don't want to start agreeing about *too* much."

"Do you know," Leah said, "somehow, I don't think that's going to be a problem."

Honk. Honk!

A big black car swept by, pulling out around the buggy with just inches to spare, blaring the horn. The Millers' normally even-tempered horse snorted and shied, jerking the buggy, hard, toward the side of the road.

Instantly Eli leaned over and placed his hands over Leah's where she held the reins, adding his strength to hers as she struggled to control the frightened horse.

"Easy, easy, now, girl," he said. "Steady. Stay steady."

The horse gave one last toss of her head and then stopped, blowing hard through her nostrils.

"Are you all right?" Eli asked.

Leah nodded. Eli relinquished his hold on the reins and got out of the buggy. "What's her name?" he asked Leah as he moved to the horse's head, speaking quietly to the animal the whole time.

"Blossom," Leah told him. She watched as he ran his hand down the horse's neck, soothing her. Leah could see that the horse was still trembling, but she was also watching Eli with interest. He let the mare sniff his hand, then he ran it down the side of her neck. Blossom nudged him with her head. A moment later, she leaned against Eli's chest.

"I think Blossom trusts you," Leah observed.

"I like horses," he said simply. He kept stroking the mare. "That's it, Blossom. There we go, girl." His voice was low and reassuring, and Leah could see the horse calming. He glanced up and met Leah's eyes. He gave a nod, as if to reassure her that everything was under control. After a few minutes, he climbed back into the buggy. The horse stood quietly.

"Danki," Leah said the moment Eli was back beside her. "She usually doesn't startle like that. I'm not sure what happened, I—"

"I know what happened," Eli said, his tone grim. "That *Englischer* honked at us on purpose."

"Well," Leah said, "thank God no harm was done." She went to lift the reins and realized that her hands were trembling. "I feel so silly!" she exclaimed. "Maybe I should just have you drive us home."

Eli's head whipped toward her as if pulled by a string. He opened his mouth to speak, closed it, then opened it again.

"I can't do that, Leah. I'm sorry."

"I don't understand."

Eli let out a long, slow breath. "You really don't know, do you?"

"No," Leah answered steadily. "Whatever it is, I do not know."

"It's because of how I hurt my leg, the reason I came to live with Victor in the first place," Eli began. "Would you just—*can* you drive? I think this would be easier if we were moving."

By way of answer, Leah checked the road behind her, and then chirruped to the horse. Her easygoing temper restored, the mare pulled the buggy back onto the road once more.

"I was in an accident, back home in Ohio," Eli continued in a quiet voice. "My best friend, Reuben, and I were buggy racing, late at night."

"Buggy racing!" Leah exclaimed, then caught herself. "I'm sorry," she said. "I didn't mean to interrupt you."

"That's all right," Eli said. "Your reaction is the sensible one. But Reuben and I didn't think of the danger, or if we did, we thought it only added to the excitement."

"What happened?"

"We took a curve too fast. The road was wet, and the buggy overturned. Both Reuben and I were thrown out. I hurt my leg, but Reuben ended up with a concussion and a broken collarbone, and his father's buggy was destroyed."

"And the horse?"

Eli's lips curved in the faintest of smiles. "The horse was fine. But after I got out of the hospital, Mamm decided I should come to live with Victor for a while. I was too wild for her to handle, she said, and I would set a bad example for the little ones."

He sent Leah a sidelong look. "You're sure you've never heard any of this before?"

"*Quite* sure," Leah answered firmly. "Nor have I heard anybody else speak of it, Eli."

"Not even your *onkel*?"

"My *onkel* John is not a gossip," Leah said.

"No," Eli acknowledged. "But Reuben's father is the bishop of our district."

"Oh," Leah said.

"So you see my point. Somebody here besides Victor must know. I thought you all did. I thought—"

"You thought we were talking about you behind your back," Leah suddenly interrupted.

"*Ja*," Eli answered shortly.

"Eli," Leah said, "no one is talking about you. Not that I know of." All of a sudden, she grinned. "Not in that way, anyhow. I *have* heard a couple of the other girls say they thought you were handsome. I didn't pay much attention, myself."

"Did you not?" Eli asked after a moment.

"No," Leah said. "I am not that kind of girl."

"No, you're not, are you?"

Leah guided Blossom up one last hill. In just a few moments, the farm stand would come into view.

"Leah," Eli suddenly said, "you should stop and let me out."

"What?"

"Stop the buggy and let me get down," Eli insisted. "I can walk the rest of the way."

Leah opened her mouth to make a smart comeback about just whose reputation Eli wanted to protect, then closed it again with a snap. She thought she knew the answer now. Without another word, she guided the buggy to the shoulder and brought it to a halt. Eli climbed down.

"Thank you again for stopping," he said. "I'll see you at the farm stand."

Before Leah could so much as utter a word, Eli strode off. Leah pulled back onto the road and completed the journey to her aunt and uncle's home. It was only as she was carrying the precious new lamp into the house that she realized she had forgotten to ask Eli what he'd been doing in town.

Ten

Miriam stood in the center of the kitchen, hands on hips, arms akimbo. Midday dinner was over, and the dishes were done. Daniel had gone back to the fields, and Sarah had walked to the farm stand to take some dinner to Leah and Eli. Miriam knew that she could follow her sister there, knew that maybe even she should. The farm stand was her responsibility now, after all. Or, if she stayed up at the house, the list of things she could be doing was at least as long as her arm.

But for the first time in as long as she could remember, the first time ever, in fact, Miriam didn't want to do anything on her usual to-do list. She didn't want to walk back and forth to the farm stand one more time. She didn't want to do a load of laundry so she could get some washing out on the line while the weather was still fine. She didn't want to do any of the things she usually did. So what was she doing?

Standing in the middle of the kitchen, doing nothing.

And it had to stop. It had to stop right now.

It seemed just a short while ago that she'd welcomed the day-to-day repetition. Now she turned in a slow circle, surveying the kitchen she so loved. How had her determination to carry on as if everything was normal become so strained?

You know the answer to that well enough, Miriam Brennemann, she thought. Everything was not normal. It wasn't normal at all.

There had been days, this past week, when Miriam could have sworn the old farmhouse, spacious as it was, had been strained to the breaking point. Because there were four of them living in the old Lapp farmhouse. Daniel, Sarah, Miriam, and Silence. A silence that grew with every passing day. A silence so enormous and profound, it all but had its own shape and form. It sat beside Miriam and Daniel at the breakfast table each morning. Put its feet up on the footstool in the living room after supper each evening. It covered Miriam and Daniel like a winter quilt when they crawled into bed each night. The weight of the silence seemed to push Miriam down into the mattress so that she could hardly summon the strength to roll over. She awoke, bleary-eyed, to muscle her way through another day until finally she had no choice but to face the truth:

The work of your hands was just work and no more if it wasn't also the work of your heart.

All of a sudden, Miriam knew exactly what she wanted to do. She left the kitchen and headed upstairs to her bedroom, taking the stairs two at a time just like she had as a child. She drew the drapes for privacy, then opened her closet and pulled out her oldest dress, the faded blue one she wore for her most hardworking chores. She changed clothes quickly then headed back downstairs.

Hurry, hurry, she thought.

She left the house, stopping in the barn to grab two buckets. Then, finally, Miriam was walking swiftly away from the house. Away from the fields where the men were working. The buckets swinging at her sides, Miriam felt her spirits lift with every step she took.

Blackberry picking. She really should have thought of this before.

An hour later Miriam stopped to stretch, raising her arms above her head and lifting her face to the afternoon sun. The day was warm. Sweat trickled down Miriam's back as she worked among the arching canes. It dampened her face and her hairline as it disappeared beneath her *kapp*, but she didn't mind. Miriam loved picking berries. She had loved it ever since she was small. When she was a girl, she'd been particularly adept at wriggling her way into the very center of the blackberry patch to find the berries the birds had left behind. She always came out scratched within an inch of her life by the canes' sharp thorns.

I am too big to do that now, she thought, though she was still grateful for her long sleeves. Even without trying to get to the center of the mass of canes, Miriam's arms would have been scratched to pieces without something to protect them. She still loved to pick, though, and this wild patch of blackberries, tucked against the flank of one of the small hills on the farm's far edge, had always been her favorite spot. She and Sarah used to come here every summer for days on end, picking until their fingers were stained purple with berry juice.

And our mouths, too, Miriam remembered with a smile. She sighed. She picked up the first bucket, nearly full now, and walked to another part of the blackberry patch, angling her body so that she could reach up high. As often as she had thought of Daniel in these last few weeks, Miriam had thought of Sarah just as often. She had so many memories of Sarah, and the truth was that most of them were happy ones. Why did those seem to want to slip away so quickly, Miriam wondered, while the memories that brought her pain held on? She pulled a handful of berries toward her, her sleeve snagging on a particularly large thorn.

"Miriam! I'm caught!"

Sarah's childish voice suddenly sounded in Miriam's mind. She froze as the memory swept over her. How old had they been that day? She could not have been more than ten, she realized, which would have made Sarah about eight. It was one of their first berry-picking expeditions on their own. Determined to reach a particularly fine specimen and so impress Daed with her skill, Sarah had ducked her head beneath a high, arching cane. But when she tried to pull her head back, she moved too quickly and the thorns caught on her *kapp* and held it fast. She could not turn around. The normally adventuresome Sarah was frightened and called out for Miriam, who quickly came running. She saw in a flash what must be done.

"Untie your *kapp*," Miriam told her sister.

"I can't! I can't move!" Sarah cried, her voice panicked.

"Don't be silly, of course you can."

"I'm not silly!" Sarah protested. "I'm smart for my age. The teacher said so."

"Then untie your *kapp*," Miriam said. "You can do it."

Sarah's fingers trembled as she fumbled with the *kapp* strings. But at last she got them undone. She wriggled out of her head covering, crouching down so that the *kapp* dangled from the cane above her head.

"Now back out slowly," Miriam instructed. "Don't hurry, Sarah, you'll just make things worse. I'm right here. I'm right behind you."

Slowly, Sarah inched her way backward out of the canes. When she was finally free of them, she spun around and threw her arms around Miriam.

"I was so scared," she said. "I didn't know where you were."

"I'm right here. I'll always be right here," Miriam had promised.

It was as if she could still feel the press of her sister's small body against hers. Feel the strength of her own arms as she and Sarah clung to each other, as if they would never let go.

Not just sisters but best friends. That was what she and Sarah had been. Of course they had both spent time with other girls, taken part in communal activities, like quilt frolics, but neither of them had ever formed a close friendship with any of the other girls around them.

We didn't have to, Miriam thought. We had each other.

For years and years, it had been Miriam and Sarah, and that had been all they needed. They played together, did chores together, walked together in the chilly mornings to the one-room schoolhouse, and sat side by side for services every Sunday. They told each other their deepest secrets. Right up until the moment that Sarah had announced that she had decided not to live the Plain life. That moment had changed the course of both their lives, and Miriam had never even had a hint that it was coming.

We had each other. That seemed to be one of the great truths of her life. *But who do we have now?*

The question popped, full-blown, into Miriam's mind. And hard on its heels, so did the answer.

God.

God was always present. He never abandoned anyone. God never changed His mind. His love was what earthly love strived to be: true, steadfast, and strong. But, also like earthly love, Miriam thought, God's love offered both shelter and a challenge. A challenge to accept that even hard times were a part of His plan. A challenge to submit to them with an open, willing heart. A heart dedicated to patient acceptance, which strived to believe that everything happened for a reason. That everything that happened under the sun, even the things that brought pain and suffering, was the work and the will of God.

Which meant that there was a reason for everything that was going on in her own life, Miriam thought. Her own current turmoil, even her unhappiness, was a part of God's plan. But why? What did God want from her? What did He want her to see that still remained hidden?

Help me, Miriam prayed. *Give me strength. Guide me, Lord.*

She reached for a cluster of berries with fingers that trembled ever so slightly.

"Miriam!" a voice behind her suddenly said. "There you are!"

Miriam jerked back, surprised. But her sleeve snagged, caught fast by the sharp blackberry thorns.

"Hold still," the voice commanded. "This will just take a second."

Sarah's long arms reached over Miriam's shoulder. With quick but careful fingers, Sarah freed the sleeve of Miriam's dress.

"Danki," Miriam said. She turned to face her sister. Sarah, too, wore old clothes, Miriam noted. Well-worn jeans and a long-sleeved T-shirt. On her feet, sensible tennis shoes with no socks.

"I'm so sorry. I didn't mean to startle you," Sarah said, her voice slightly breathless, as if she had hurried all the way to the blackberry patch. All of a sudden, she smiled. "But at least it wasn't your *kapp*! Do you remember—"

"I do." Miriam nodded before Sarah could finish. "It's funny you should mention that day. I was just thinking about it."

"I can't believe you came out here without me," Sarah went on. "Why didn't you come down to the stand to get me? Why didn't you tell me you were going?"

"I didn't know I was going until I actually did it," Miriam confessed. "I was just standing in the kitchen and suddenly none of my usual chores seemed right. Then I remembered it was blackberry season, and the next thing I knew, here I was."

"And you've been busy, too," Sarah said. She leaned over to peer into Miriam's bucket, nearly full now. "Never mind. I'll just have to work twice as hard to catch up." She straightened up, her face alight with mischief. "Wanna bet I can do it?"

"Sarah," Miriam protested, surprised to hear the thread of laughter in her own voice. "You know I never bet."

"That doesn't mean I can't do it," Sarah answered with a smile. She hoisted her bucket and moved a short distance away, near enough so that she and Miriam could still speak to each other, but not so close that they would be working side by side.

"And I'll tell you something else, Miriam Brennemann," she called, her own voice filled with laughter now. "Sometimes I think you seriously need to lighten up."

"Sarah, slow down!" Miriam protested some time later. The sun was climbing high now, and sweat trickled down her back. She continued to pick at a leisurely, steady pace, but Sarah had done her best to work twice as fast. "It's not a race."

"Don't be ridiculous. Of course it is," Sarah replied. "Sometimes I think I've been trying to catch up to you my whole life."

Partway through the act of hefting her bucket to move to a different spot, Miriam stopped abruptly.

"What?" she asked. She straightened and turned toward the sound of Sarah's voice. When her sister didn't answer, she walked around the blackberry patch until Sarah came into view. "What did you just say?"

"I only meant that you were older, that's all," Sarah said. But she did not stop picking, and she did not meet Miriam's eyes. "Younger siblings always try to catch up. It's just the way things are."

"No," Miriam said. "I don't think that's what you meant at all. Why would you even say a thing like that?"

"I said it because it's true! Why else?" Sarah snapped. She stopped picking berries and ran a hand across her forehead, as if it ached. Her fingers left a faint blue streak. "I'm sorry," she said. "I didn't come out here to quarrel."

"Why did you come?" Miriam asked.

"Because I wanted to see you!" Sarah exclaimed. "Is that so odd? I wanted to talk to you. You're always so busy these days, but, except for down at the farm stand, you never let me help." She sighed and ran a hand through her blond hair, pushing it back from her face. "I thought it would be like old times, coming back to stay for a while. But it's not like that. It hasn't been like that at all. Some of it is because Daed died, of course, but for the rest . . . sometimes I think you wish I'd never come at all."

"I never said that," Miriam insisted, but even she barely believed her own words. True, she had never said it, but how many times had she thought it?

Sarah gave a derisive snort. "No, you haven't. I'll give

you that much. But I'm not stupid, you know. Just because I live among the *Englischers* now doesn't mean I can't tell when something's wrong. You've been angry with me for weeks, Miriam, but I'll be darned if I know why. I was hoping we could be sisters, just like we've always been. Apparently, I was wrong."

"And just because I'm Plain doesn't make me stupid, either," Miriam replied, stung. "I *am* your sister. I'll always be your sister. But you can't just waltz back in here like nothing's changed. It has. And I don't just mean Daed dying. You changed things yourself, the day that you left."

"And you've never forgiven me for that, have you?" Sarah demanded, swinging to face Miriam fully now. "You blame me for leaving home." She stopped for a moment, studying her sister's face, then said in a calmer tone, "Daed understood and accepted it. Why can't you accept me the way I am now?"

"I do accept you as you are," Miriam said, trying to make her voice equally calm. "You didn't give us much choice in that, did you? There you are, thousands of miles away, living among the *Englischers*, wearing jeans and talking on a cell phone, as if you were not brought up Plain, as if our way means nothing to you."

Sarah shook her head, suddenly looking old beyond her years. "That's it, then," she said. "You think I did something unforgivable when I left. And that the way I live my life is wrong. You think I'm a bad person now."

"I don't think you're a bad person," Miriam cried. "Stop putting words in my mouth!"

"Then what's the matter with you?" Sarah all but shouted. "What's the matter with *us*, Miriam? Why can't we talk? We used to be so close."

"I'm not the one who changed that," Miriam came right back.

"There! See? You *do* blame me!" Sarah pounced.

"No!" Miriam countered, growing heated in turn. "How many times do I have to say it? I don't. But I've never understood how you could do such a thing. How could you leave us, Daed and me? How could you walk out and leave your whole life behind?"

And how could you make that decision without telling me? You never shared your thoughts. Not once.

Sarah's expression softened, and Miriam saw both sympathy and sadness in her eyes. "You make it sound like I was willful and rebellious." She gave a small, unhappy laugh. "Or like I gave up my life here for cell phones and jeans. But that's not how it was. It was far simpler than that. I had no choice, Miriam. I followed the path laid out for me by God."

Miriam flushed. It was as if a fire raced through all her veins. "How can you say such a thing?" she gasped. "How can abandoning the way you were raised be God's will?"

"That's simple, too," Sarah answered, but suddenly she sounded exhausted. "I didn't abandon anything, Miriam. In fact, I tried to take as much with me as I could. I'm still trying. That's the whole point."

"What point?" Miriam asked, pushing down a surge of frustration. "I don't understand," she said. "I don't understand anything about this. I don't understand *you* anymore."

"That makes us even, then," Sarah said. "Because these last few weeks, I don't understand you, either."

Unexpectedly, Sarah sat down. Miriam hesitated, and then moved to sit facing her sister, cross-legged, her knees bumping against Sarah's. They had often sat just this way when they were small. For several moments, neither of them spoke. Miriam felt the sun, warm on her back. The blackberry canes rustled ever so slightly as the wind moved through them. She heard a bird call, high overhead. But she did not speak. Sarah had started this. It was up to her to speak first.

"Do you remember that game we used to play when we were little," Sarah finally asked, "the one we called Close Your Eyes?"

"Of course I remember it," Miriam answered, though she had not thought of this game in a very long time.

It was Sarah who had originally created it as a way to help conquer her fear of thunderstorms. Though Miriam had never been much interested in games of imagination, she had been frightened enough by thunderstorms herself to be more than happy to play along.

Whenever a storm got too close, whipping the trees in the yard by the house into a frenzy, the thunder booming loud enough to shake the walls of their bedroom, the lightning so bright it made the whole yard look like day, the sisters would huddle together under the bedcovers and close their eyes. The game was to imagine you were someplace else, anyplace else, as long as there was no thunderstorm. It could be a place you knew or one that your mind conjured up out of nothing.

Miriam had never traveled very far in her imagination. In fact, she hadn't really traveled at all. Most of the time the place she conjured up was her very own room, her very own bed. She just subtracted the thunderstorm. But Sarah had imagined all sorts of places when she closed her eyes. Places that, even as a child, Miriam had known that she could never go.

"When I was trying to understand what I should do," Sarah went on softly, "whether I should stay and live a Plain life or go and live among the *Englischers*, I played a sort of grown-up version of Close Your Eyes."

"You played a *game*?" Miriam said, aghast. "To make the most important decision of your life?"

"I didn't think of it as a game," Sarah said, and Miriam could hear the effort her sister was making not to sound defensive. "I thought of it as—I don't know—a way to focus. To shut out all the distractions of the here and now and try to imagine the future.

"I thought—if I could just see some part of it, even if it was only one image, then I would know what I should do. I would know where I belonged."

"And did you see something?" Miriam asked, her own voice quiet now.

"Yes," Sarah said softly. "Yes, I did."

"What?"

"Nothing. Nothing at all."

Miriam tried to imagine that. If she had been the one to see that nothing, she would have been paralyzed with fear, caught in terrifying dread. She had always known where she belonged. Here, in the community in which she was raised, in the house where she had grown up. What must it have been like to see only a great emptiness where the future was supposed to be?

"That must have been terrible," she said.

Sarah gave a short, unamused laugh. "It was. I don't think I've ever been so scared in my life, if you must know. It was as if God were telling me I didn't have a future. I suppose if I'd been less . . ." Sarah paused, as if struggling to find the right word.

"Stubborn?" Miriam suggested and was rewarded with Sarah's quick smile.

"Okay, stubborn," Sarah acknowledged. "I'd have stopped trying so hard. Accepted the fact that the reason I couldn't see anything meant that there was nothing *to* see. That what was important was what was right in front of me when I *opened* my eyes. But I *was* too stubborn. You're absolutely right about that. So I kept on trying, over and over, night after night. And then, one night, when I closed my eyes and no image came to me, I realized that I wasn't afraid anymore. That was the night I thought I understood.

"The reason I couldn't picture the future was because I was supposed to go someplace I'd never been before."

Miriam sat still, trying to digest her sister's words. How brave Sarah was! she realized. To keep doing what made her afraid, night after night, never being certain she would ever see an outcome, let alone a positive one.

"What finally happened?" she asked quietly. "Did you ever see anything at all?"

Sarah gave another quick laugh, more open and free this time.

"Yes," she said. "It's going to sound like pride, but the moment I realized I'd stopped being afraid, the thing I saw was myself. I still couldn't see my surroundings, but I could see myself, very clearly, and I was walking forward, as if there was a path all laid out for me, as if it had been there all the time. It just took letting go of my fear to see it. I *did* have a future, but I would have to make it for myself. The only thing I would take from my old life would be . . . me. Not just my body, but also my heart and soul. What I had learned, what I believed. And it seemed to me that I could not have seen or felt these things on my own. God must be guiding me. This was the path He wanted me to walk."

"But why choose to live among the *Englischers*?" Miriam asked. "Why go so far away? There are Mennonite communities close by. You could have just gone there."

But Sarah was already shaking her head.

"No. It had to be someplace totally new."

"But *why*?"

"Because of who I am, I think," Sarah said. She wiped a hand across her face once more, leaving a trace of blue on her cheek this time. "Because I was raised Plain."

Miriam laughed. "Now you have me more confused than ever."

"You remember when we were having supper with Daniel's parents?" Sarah asked. "And I was talking about teaching the young people how to garden? I wish that you could meet some of them, Miriam. At first, they seem so angry. But get to know them just a little and you see the truth: They're lost. They have no sense of fellowship, not with others, and not within themselves. I sometimes think this is the biggest difference between the Plain folk and the *Englischers*. We don't want to be connected to the outside world. But, for all their laptops and cell phones, the *Englischers* have forgotten how to be connected to one another and to themselves."

Sarah paused. Miriam gazed at her sister's face. All the anger and frustration in it was gone. Instead, Sarah's face was filled with strength and purpose, with a glowing inner light.

"But you should see what happens when these young people see the first shoots come out of the soil!" she went on. "It's like the whole world opens up. They realize that life has possibilities—that they, themselves, have possibilities—for the very first time. You can almost see the desire for fellowship grow just as quickly as the carrot tops!

"This is what God wants me to do," Sarah said, her voice ringing with conviction. "He wants me to bring this sense of fellowship to the *Englischers*, particularly the young people. This is what I believe, Miriam. I believe it with my whole heart."

"Did Daed know this?" Miriam whispered.

"Yes." Sarah nodded, and now a shadow crossed her face. "At least, in part. He didn't know about the job, of course, and for that I will always be sorry. That *was* pride. I wanted so much to tell Daed in person. I wanted to be able to see the expression on his face when I told of my accomplishments. That was wrong of me. I think I even knew it at the time. But, after I told him I did not wish to be baptized, I did my best to explain why I felt I had to go."

"But you didn't tell me," Miriam said.

Sarah met Miriam's eyes. In them, Miriam saw the glint of tears. She felt her own eyes fill.

"I wanted to," Sarah said. "You have no idea how much. But I simply did not know how. Something came between us, Miriam, even before I decided to leave home. There were days when I swore I could almost see you stepping back, stepping away from me, once you had been baptized. It was as if you were trying to put as much distance between the two of us as possible."

"No," Miriam protested. "It wasn't like that at all."

But it was, she thought. Until Sarah had spoken, Miriam had had absolutely no idea that her sister was considering leaving the Plain life. But she had been sure, so very sure, that Daniel wanted to ask Sarah to become his wife.

I did step back, Miriam realized. Not to hurt her sister, only to put some distance between herself and the pain she was so sure would come. It never had. Not in the form that she'd expected, anyhow. Sarah had gone to live among the *Englischers.* Daniel had asked Miriam to be his wife. And for all the days between that one and this, Miriam had lived with the pain that came with the belief that she had been her husband's second choice.

And I can't tell Sarah any of this, she thought. *Not here. Not now.* Sarah had just revealed a story full of faith and hope. How could Miriam reveal one of pain and unrequited love? She could not. She would not. But she could do something else.

"I'm sorry," she said quietly. "I never meant to hurt you, Sarah. And I"—Miriam's breath caught—"I've missed you so much! Particularly once we knew how sick Daed was."

"I should have been here," Sarah said as the tears began to slide down her cheeks. "I should have been here to help, and I should have been with Daed when he died."

"He *was* proud of you," Miriam said, her own tears spilling over. "He saved every letter you ever sent. He read them over and over. He might not have known about your job, the wonderful work you are doing, but I think he understood, Sarah. In his heart, you had his full support. No matter where you were or how you chose to live, you always had his love."

"Thank you," Sarah whispered. "Thank you, Miriam."

She leaned forward and threw her arms around Miriam's neck. Fiercely, Miriam returned her sister's hug. All the pain, the uncertainty about her relationship with Daniel, seemed to fade into the background. How she had misjudged Sarah and her reasons for leaving home! But this, at least, she could repair. She could assure her sister of her love. She gave Sarah one last squeeze, and then let go. The two sisters sat back.

"Oh, no!" Sarah cried. She began to laugh, though the tears continued to slip down her cheeks. "I think I got blackberry juice on you."

Miriam laughed, too. "Never mind. It will fit right in with what I put there myself." She got to her feet. "It's getting late. We should go home."

Sarah scrambled to her feet, then surveyed her bucket with a mournful expression. "You beat me," she said. "You have twice as many berries as I do. But then, you had a head start."

"They're all going to end up in the same place anyway,"

Miriam observed as she and Sarah hefted their buckets and walked to where Miriam had left her second one.

"Spoken like a true Plain woman," Sarah said with a smile. "Here, let me carry that." She caught the second bucket by the handle and lifted it up. "What's for supper? Do we have time to make pies?"

"There's always time to make pie," Miriam observed. "And *that* is spoken like a true Plain woman."

"It is," Sarah said. "It is, indeed."

Obeying an impulse, Miriam slipped her free arm through Sarah's. Linked together now, the sisters walked arm in arm through the late afternoon sunshine.

Eleven

"I know," Sarah said as they approached the house, "let's make pies."

"I thought we settled that," Miriam answered. "Of course we will make pies."

"No," Sarah said with a quick shake of her head. "I mean, let's do it now, for supper tonight. Let's each make a pie. And then . . ." Sarah's face lit up with mischief. "Let's see if Daniel can tell them apart!"

Do I dare? Miriam wondered. How clearly she could picture in her mind's eye the scene she hoped for. Daniel sitting at the table, two seemingly identical slices of pie in front of him. He would regard them with his usual serious, intent expression. He would take a bite of one piece of pie and then the other, savoring each, chewing slowly. Perhaps he would even close his eyes to better experience the flavors that filled his mouth. Then he would take one more bite, just for good measure.

"This one is yours, Miriam," he would say, gesturing to the correct pie. "I would know it anywhere." And then he would smile, and Miriam would feel her heart soar. "I would know it anywhere because I love you. Because you are my wife."

"Miriam." Sarah's voice cut across Miriam's daydream. "Where did you go?"

"To the kitchen," Miriam answered with a quick laugh, though she did not explain more.

"Is that a yes to the pie contest?" Sarah asked.

Miriam nodded. "Definitely. Yes."

Back at the house, Miriam and Sarah worked quickly and efficiently, effortlessly falling back into the rhythms that had filled their childhood. Miriam measured dry ingredients for crust into two bowls while Sarah gently rinsed the berries, setting them in a colander to drain away the excess water. Then the sisters stood side by side, making their crusts. They let the pie dough rest for a few minutes while they measured out their berries and added sugar and spices. Sarah had a heavier hand with the cinnamon, Miriam noted.

Then they let the berries sit to let the thickening begin while they rolled out the pie crusts. Finally, each sister gently scooped the berries into her shell and settled the upper crust on top.

"I forgot how much I like pie making," Sarah observed as she crimped the edges, sealing the top and bottom crusts together and giving the pie a festive look all at the same time.

"I like it, too," Miriam agreed. The dry feel of the flour on her hands, the scents of ripe fruit and spices. "How many vents do you want to cut?"

"Five," Sarah answered at once. "I always think an odd number looks better, don't you?"

"I do," Miriam agreed.

Using just the tip of a sharp knife, she made five short incisions in the top crust of her pie, to let the air escape so the top crust wouldn't puff up. When the juices began to bubble through the vents, Miriam would know that the pie was done. She handed the knife to Sarah. Frowning a little in concentration, Sarah placed five similar cuts on her pie top.

"There!" she said. The sisters stood back, admiring their handiwork. The two pies really did look identical. "Not bad!" She giggled. "I can't wait to see the look on Daniel's face."

"I'll just pop them in the oven," Miriam said. She placed the two pies on a large cookie sheet so that no juice would drip onto the oven floor.

"I'm so sticky!" Sarah exclaimed. "Do you want help washing up?"

"No, that's okay," Miriam answered. "You go on and get cleaned up. I'll get supper started and get these bowls washed up."

"Thanks," Sarah said. She put an arm around Miriam's shoulders and gave a quick squeeze. "That was fun."

"It *was* fun," Miriam admitted. Sarah turned and headed toward the door that led to the rest of the house. "Sarah."

Sarah stopped and turned around. "What?"

"I'm glad that you are home."

"I'm happy, too," Sarah said. "See you in a few minutes. Leave something for me to do, now. Even if it's just setting the table."

"Oh, you can definitely do that," Miriam said. Setting the table had always been Miriam's least favorite job.

Sarah was laughing as she sprinted through the door. Miriam could hear her sister's footsteps thundering up the stairs. She smiled. How many times had Daed asked Sarah not to take the stairs at a dead run? she wondered. So many there was no way to count them all. Sarah had managed to slow down for a time or two, but somehow, she'd always ended up running once more. It seemed she had always been going somewhere, even as a child.

Miriam put the bowls, sticky with their residue of sugar and berry juices, in the sink, then quickly began to wash them. She was sticky as well, and still sweaty from the berry picking. She, too, would need washing. Miriam stopped, one hand still in the dishwater, as inspiration struck. Then she was moving before she could change her mind. Through the kitchen door and out into the yard. As she often did when she worked in the house, Miriam had kicked her shoes off the moment she came indoors. The lush grass was cool and soft beneath her feet as she made her way to the pump in the yard.

Miriam worked the handle quickly to create a good, steady flow. Then she released the pump handle and thrust both hands into the water, gasping at how cold it was. But it felt so good! No amount of water would wash away the berry stains, not yet anyhow. But the water flowed over Miriam's tired hands, making them tingle. She splashed some water upward, onto her face, and laughed aloud.

Do I dare? she wondered, then answered her own question by pumping the handle, hard, once more. Water gushed from the spout. Pulling in a deep breath, Miriam did what she had so often seen Daniel do at the end of a hot day: She thrust her face directly beneath the flow.

Miriam sputtered as the cold water streamed across her face. Daniel had a definite advantage, she realized. He only had to try to keep the front of his shirt dry. Miriam had the front of her dress and her *kapp* as well. She pulled back and shook her head. *Just like a dog,* she thought. Then she laughed aloud.

"You can never tease me about doing that again, you know."

Miriam straightened up with a start. She had been so caught up in what she was doing that she had not heard Daniel approach. He stood now, on the far side of the pump, a grin on his face and a very definite twinkle in his bright blue eyes. With a suddenness that had her head spinning, Miriam felt her heart soar. How long had it been since Daniel had looked at her with such an expression of open joy? She genuinely did not know. But how much she wanted to keep it there, that Miriam knew very well.

Her hand was moving almost of its own volition, before Miriam was conscious of making a decision to act at all. It was scooping down into the water trough, and then back up, sending a great arc of water *whooshing* in Daniel's direction, striking him full in the chest, darkening his shirt front. Daniel gave an exclamation of astonishment. And then incredibly, wonderfully, he was laughing. A great, full-throated laugh that rang out across the yard.

"I hope you don't expect to get away with that," he said. He took a step forward. Miriam skittered back, keeping the water trough between them.

"Race you back to the house."

She turned to go, but almost before she finished pivoting, Daniel was at her side. Reaching out to seize her by the hand.

"No, let's go together," he said.

"Let's," Miriam agreed, her heart so full she thought it just might burst with joy.

Hand in hand, they raced across the yard.

Miriam didn't think she could ever remember a supper like the one they shared that night. The joyous mood continued throughout the meal, catching Sarah up in it the moment she came downstairs. It was as if all three of them had stepped into the sunshine, Miriam thought, bursting through after weeks of standing beneath dark clouds.

"*Ach*, Sarah, surely you must have another slice of bread," Daniel said after he had helped himself to the green beans. "Is it not good enough to eat two slices?"

Sarah laughed at the suggestion. "I've already eaten three, and I've had two helpings of the potato salad, so please don't urge me to eat a third." She looked at her brother-in-law and shook her head. "In the *Englischer* world, you could simply tell your wife that her cooking is delicious."

"Doesn't that lead to pride?" Miriam said at once.

"Maybe," Sarah said. "But it's also a more . . . direct way of telling someone that you enjoy the food she's cooked for you. Is there anything so terrible in that?"

"No," Daniel answered. He looked straight at Miriam. "I do enjoy it," he said. "I'm lucky to have a wife who cooks such food."

Miriam felt herself blushing to the roots of her hair beneath her *kapp*. "Thank you, Daniel," she said. "I am glad my cooking pleases you." It was a small thing, but Daniel's words had filled her heart with joy.

"And how is the work in the fields coming?" she asked him, realizing that ever since her *daed* had died, she had shown very little interest in her husband's work. If there had been distance between them, she was at least partly to blame.

"Good," he said, seeming pleased that she had asked. "We have more corn this summer than we've had in years. It will be a bountiful harvest."

When the meal was over, it was Sarah who got up to clear the table while Miriam put on a pot of coffee. While it brewed, Miriam got out dessert plates and, finally, the pies.

"I thought I smelled pie," Daniel said as Miriam and Sarah each carried a pie to the table and set them in front of him. He gazed at them, his expression slightly bemused. "But I don't think even I can eat two."

"You don't have to eat all of them," Sarah said, her voice teasing. "Just a couple of bites of each one."

Daniel raised his eyes to Sarah's face. "You're going to cut both pies at once? But why?"

"It's a game," Sarah explained. "Or maybe a quiz. I don't know. I baked one pie and Miriam baked the other."

Daniel's gaze shifted to Miriam, a faint frown snaking down between his brows. Miriam felt a fine tingling start in the pit of her stomach.

"More pie is always a blessing," Daniel said carefully. "But I'm still not certain that I understand."

"Daniel," Sarah said, her tone both amused and exasperated, "you're working too hard. Here . . . let me just . . ."

Swiftly, Sarah cut a piece from each pie, slid them onto the waiting plates, and then placed the plates in front of Daniel.

"Now," she went on, setting a fork down on the table with a sharp *click*, "take a bite of each and see if you can tell which one is Miriam's and which one is mine."

"You are testing me," Daniel said in a strange, flat voice. A voice that Miriam had never heard him use before. Again, his eyes sought out her face, and this time Miriam felt her stomach plummet.

He's looking at me as if I'm a stranger, she thought, her sense of pleasure at the meal rapidly turning to dismay.

"You agreed to this?" Daniel asked. "This is what you want?"

"Oh, but"—Miriam faltered—"surely Sarah is right. You're making this too hard. We both wanted to bake a pie, and we thought it would be fun to see if you could tell them apart. It's just a game. That's all."

"No," Daniel said. He got to his feet. "It is not a game. It is vanity. It is pride. Perhaps I should not be surprised that Sarah would propose such a thing, she has lived among the *Englischers* for so long."

Sarah made a sound of protest, but Daniel went right on. "But I am surprised at you, Miriam. How can you not see that this is wrong? How can you be in fellowship and competition at the same time?"

"You can't," Miriam admitted softly, her voice all but breaking. The evening had been such a gift, such an *unexpected* gift, she thought. And now she had spoiled it; she had ruined it all. No wonder Daniel looked at her as if she were a stranger. Miriam had forgotten who, and what, she was.

She was a Plain woman, and she had no place putting her husband, or anyone else, to the test.

"You are right, Daniel," she said. More than anything in the world, Miriam wanted to hide her face, but she made herself look straight into her husband's eyes. "I apologize."

Something came into Daniel's eyes then, a thing Miriam could no longer gaze upon, for if she did, she knew she would not be able to hold back the tears. She dropped her eyes. In front of her, on the table, were the two pies. Miriam leaned over and picked them up. She carried them to the counter, then returned for the plates with their single slices.

"Miriam," Sarah protested softly. "It was my idea. It's unfair of Daniel to blame you so."

"No," Miriam said, in a calm and careful voice. "It doesn't matter who thought of it as long as I agreed to take part. Daniel is right." She turned back toward the sink. "I don't know about either of you," she went on, "but I have lost my taste for pie tonight."

"Well, I haven't," Sarah said. She seized one of the plates, taking it out of Miriam's hands, and marched smartly out the kitchen door. It closed behind her with a bang, leaving Miriam and Daniel alone.

"Do you need help with the dishes?" Daniel asked, a question Miriam could never remember him posing before. Doing dishes was woman's work.

"No, *danki*," Miriam replied. "I can manage on my own." She turned and extended the piece of pie she still held toward her husband. "It's blackberry," she said, as if this were a thing Daniel could not see perfectly well for himself. "Sarah and I picked all afternoon. I'll start on the jam first thing tomorrow."

"Miriam," Daniel said, "you are working too hard."

"No harder than you are," Miriam replied.

She turned back toward the sink, still clutching the plate with its single slice of pie. As if from a great distance, her brain sent a message—*Put it down*—but Miriam seemed frozen. She could not get her arm to comply.

"I'll just go try and get caught up on the farm journals, then," Daniel finally said.

"Ja, gut," Miriam answered. "I know it troubles you to be behind."

For a moment, she thought Daniel would say something

more. But he turned and vanished into the house, leaving Miriam alone.

The rest of the evening passed in a strange blur. The details of the tasks she performed stood out, clear as day, but it seemed to Miriam that the world beyond the scope of her hands had simply ceased to exist. Daniel had ceased to exist. She could not reach him anymore.

Miriam did the dishes, gently wiping them dry and putting them away with such care they made no noise even as she set one plate atop another. The dishes done, she got out her canning supplies in preparation for making jam tomorrow. She checked the jars to make sure the rims were free of cracks. She matched the number of jars to rings and lids, making certain she had enough to go around. She would wash them tomorrow. The jars needed to be clean and hot when the jam went into them, so there was no sense in doing it tonight. She was lining the supplies up into meticulously neat rows on the kitchen counter when Sarah came back in through the kitchen door. A waft of sweetly scented evening air blew in with her. In her hand, Sarah carried her now-empty plate and fork.

"Miriam," she said as she took in the kitchen. "You should have let me help."

"It's all right," Miriam said, not turning. "I'm fine."

"Miriam," Sarah said again. She moved to put her plate in the sink and then stepped to Miriam's side, placing a hand upon her arm. "How can you say such things? It isn't

171

all right. And you're not fine. I can see that for myself. Let me talk to Daniel," Sarah urged. "Let me explain. It's unfair that he should blame you when it's really all my fault."

"No." Miriam shook her head. "Daniel is right. It was a foolish idea, and I should not have taken part."

"But . . ." Sarah began.

Miriam gripped the counter edge so tightly, the knuckles of her hands showed white. "Please," she whispered. "Please, Sarah, just let it go. No more tonight."

Miriam felt her sister's hand drop away. "If you're sure," Sarah said, her voice still troubled. "Miriam, I wish you would let me—"

"I am sure," Miriam said forcefully. "I appreciate your offer, honestly I do, but this is between Daniel and me now."

"I'll see you tomorrow morning, then," Sarah said. She turned to go. "You'll probably have to lend me an apron," she said from the kitchen doorway. "You remember what I'm like when it comes to making jam."

"I remember," Miriam said softly.

But she did not turn. A few moments later, she heard Sarah's footsteps recede into the house. Sarah had to pass through the living room to reach the stairs to the second story, but Miriam did not hear her sister wish Daniel good night. Nor did she hear Daniel go upstairs. Had he already gone up to their room?

Miriam put off leaving the kitchen for as long as she could, but finally even she could find nothing more that needed to be done. Besides, she couldn't put off facing Daniel forever. Squaring her shoulders, Miriam headed for the living room. It was empty. But there was a kerosene lamp burning on the table by her favorite chair. Slowly, her legs feeling wooden, Miriam walked over and sank just as slowly down into the chair.

Whose kindness was responsible for the light? she wondered. Was it Daniel or Sarah who had left it burning for her? Just for a moment, Miriam leaned back in the chair, resting her head against its high back. Hands clasped loosely in her lap, Miriam closed her eyes. She could feel the old farmhouse settling all around her, whispering and sighing to itself as it began to let go of the heat of the day and welcome in the cool air of night.

I want to be like this house, she thought. *Patient and enduring. Able to let things come and go.* But even as she made the wish, she knew that it would never come true. She might learn to endure, but she would never truly be patient. She longed for too much. And how could she learn to let go of something she had never been certain had ever been hers to start with? How could she let go of longing for her own husband's love?

She winced as she thought of Daniel's reaction to the pie contest. She had been so happy, had felt so close to him, and seconds later, he shamed her. *I was wrong,* she admitted, *but if he really loved me, he wouldn't have rebuked me that way, especially not in front of Sarah.* Her mind circled back to the awful possibility. *Perhaps he doesn't love me. And who could blame him? What kind of wife is unable to give her husband children? And how does any man come to love a wife who's his second choice?*

Miriam realized she had drawn her knees up to her chest and was hugging them to her, as if to shield herself from all the grief she felt, for her marriage, for herself.

For a short, sweet time today, she had believed that things were getting better between her and Daniel. Instead, everything was so much worse.

I cannot bear this, she thought.

Miriam opened her eyes. There was something else she could not do. She couldn't put off facing the consequences of her own actions any longer. Pushing up from the chair, she turned down the light.

Daniel was sitting in the chair by the window in their bedroom, his face illuminated by the soft glow of lamplight, a tidy stack of farm journals at his feet. He looked up as Miriam came into the room.

"You were a long time," he observed quietly.

"Sarah and I will make jam tomorrow," Miriam said. She walked to her dressing table, fingers fumbling with her *kapp* strings. "I wanted to make sure everything was ready. It will be good if we can get going early, before it gets too hot."

"She didn't help you with the preparations?"

"It's all right," Miriam said quickly, suddenly moved to defend her sister. She sat down at her dressing table and turned up the lamp. The bowl was warm. "I don't mind. Sarah has other things she needs to do and I . . ." Miriam removed her *kapp* and placed it on the dressing table. "We're not the same, Sarah and I."

"I know that, Miriam," Daniel said softly.

Miriam's breath caught in her throat. For one terrible moment, she feared that she might cry. Quickly, she began to remove the pins from her hair, setting them in the dish she kept on the dressing table for just this purpose. They made soft pinging sounds as they landed.

And then, with a suddenness that made her gasp with relief, Miriam's hair was down. Freed from its pins and the tight coil in which it was confined all day, it rippled down her back, thick, luxurious, golden. On their wedding night, the first time Daniel had taken her hair into his hands, he had gazed at it in wonder and then said that it was like holding a spill of sunshine.

Abruptly, Miriam realized that her head ached. The lamplight hurt her eyes. Although she'd turned it up just moments before, now Miriam reached to turn it down again, then decided to simply blow it out.

In the darkened room, she burrowed her fingers into her hair, pressing her fingertips against her scalp. *Breathe. Just breathe,* she thought. She reached for her hairbrush. As she did, Daniel's hand came down to cover hers.

"Your head hurts, doesn't it?" he asked.

Miriam jumped. She'd been so taken up with keeping her emotions contained that she hadn't noticed that Daniel had gotten up and come to stand behind her. She nodded.

"Yes, it does."

"Let me brush your hair," Daniel said. "That usually helps, doesn't it?"

Again, Miriam nodded. But she could not bring herself to speak this time. Slowly, she slid her hand out from under

Daniel's. He lifted the brush. A moment later, Miriam felt the stiff bristles ease through her hair and then glide along her scalp. She closed her eyes.

Oh, but it was glorious! Daniel hands were gentle yet sure as he lifted Miriam's hair and slid the brush through it over and over again, in a steady, even rhythm that had the pain easing from her head, neck, and shoulders almost from the very first stroke. The room around them was peaceful and still. A faint breath of air brushed against Miriam's shins. She could hear Daniel breathing in the same rhythm with which he stroked the brush through her hair. In time to the beating of Miriam's own heart.

How I wish it could always be like this! she thought. If only she could always feel so close to Daniel. So much, so very much in love.

"I am sorry for your pain, Miriam," Daniel said.

Miriam jerked beneath his hands. In spite of herself, she made a soft, inarticulate sound. He was trying to be kind, but that wasn't enough. It wasn't kindness she needed. It was for Daniel to love and desire her as wholly as she loved him. Miriam pulled in a breath and felt it move in her chest like the twist of a knife.

"Stop," she gasped out. "Please, Daniel."

Daniel's fingers stilled at once. "What is it?" he asked. "What's wrong?"

"I'm sorry," Miriam said. "I'm sorry. It's just . . . this isn't helping after all."

Just for a moment, Daniel stood without moving, still so close that Miriam could feel the heat of his body. She gripped her hands tightly together in her lap, desperately

176

fighting for control. Her fingers were icy cold. Then he set the hairbrush down on the dressing table with a sharp *click*.

"I'm sorry, too," he said. He took a step back. "I will say good night."

Without another word he walked to his chair and extinguished the light, plunging the room into darkness. A moment later, Miriam heard the soft creak of the bed as Daniel lay down. She sat at her dressing table, head in her hands, until she thought she heard his breathing become smooth and even. Only then did she rise. She changed into her nightclothes, draping her work clothes over the back of her chair. They would be perfect for making jam in the following morning. Finally, Miriam moved on silent feet toward the bed. She held her breath for a moment as she slipped between the sheets, but Daniel did not stir.

As he had from their first night together as husband and wife, Daniel slept on the side of the bed closest to the window, his body turned so that his face was angled toward it. Miriam had teased him about it, during those first few weeks of marriage, claiming that Daniel was so eager to get to work he slept so that he could see the first rays of sun.

Sometimes, in the years that followed, Miriam had wished that Daniel would turn around. That he would sleep with his face toward her, as if she were his sun and it was her face that he longed to see the instant he opened his eyes. She wished that he would turn to her, spontaneously, in the night and hold her in his arms. He never did, though. Instead, when she was troubled and unable to sleep, Miriam had taken to laying her hand against Daniel's back. Not a caress, simply a touch. A way to feel his skin against hers, to be connected to his solidity and warmth. She had never known if Daniel was aware of what she did or not.

Now, lying beside him in the bed they had shared for six long years, in the bed where they had tried without success for all those years to conceive a child, Miriam did not reach out. Instead, she rolled over, clinging to the side of the bed.

It was a very long time before she closed her eyes.

Twelve

S ummer is a remarkable season of the year," Bishop John said at worship that Sunday. "We see God's work, His bounty, everywhere we look. But this bounty brings with it a special challenge. A challenge to remember to give thanks for all that we are given, to not become so wrapped up in the hard work it takes to keep our farms and businesses going that we forget that we cannot, we do not, accomplish this work alone.

"We need the support of those who work beside us, our families and friends. And, always, we need God. We need His guidance and strength. Sometimes I think we need it in this season of bounty most of all. Because with bounty can come distraction, even complacency. It is easy to ask for God's help when the days are cold and difficult, but less easy to offer up thanks when they are bright and warm.

"And so, as we prepare to recite the Lord's Prayer in the silence of our minds and hearts, let us do so in a true spirit of thanksgiving, remembering that even the strongest hands will falter if they are not guided by a heart that is dedicated to, and humble before, God. Let us pray."

Seated just behind Rachel and Leah, Miriam bowed her head and closed her eyes. As so often happened when Bishop John spoke, she felt as if his words were meant specifically for her.

I need to give thanks, she thought. The farm stand was prospering. Although her father was gone, he was with God, and Miriam still lived in the house she loved so much. And she was who she had always wanted to be. She was Daniel Brennemann's wife. The fact that being his wife had not turned out to be quite what she had imagined did not make the gift of her marriage any less precious.

Perhaps I have been wrong about my imagination all these years, she suddenly thought. *Perhaps it isn't that I have too little, but that I have too much.*

Too much to give thanks for things precisely as they were. For life precisely as it was, with all its pain and flaws.

Give us this day our daily bread, and forgive us our trespasses as we forgive those who trespass against us, she prayed. Even if the one who trespassed against her most was Miriam herself.

"Here, let me take that," Miriam offered. She held out her hands for the plate of sandwiches Victor King's wife, Rebecca, had just lifted from the kitchen counter. "It looks heavy."

"It is!" Rebecca admitted with a smile. She relinquished the plate, then pressed her hands into the small of her back. The action thrust her pregnant belly forward even more. "I get so tired lately. I admit, I will be happy when this baby comes."

"You should sit down," Miriam suggested. "Aren't you near your time?"

"Early September," Rebecca said. She lifted a smaller plate, of cookies this time, with a laugh. "Less than a month and not nearly soon enough!"

Miriam smiled. Rebecca shot her a quick look, and Miriam could feel herself brace. *Here it comes,* she thought. Some well-meaning remark about how hard it must be for Miriam because she and Daniel were still childless.

"I hope that Eli is behaving himself."

"He's doing more than that," Miriam replied, grateful that it was Eli who was the topic of conversation. She held the door for Rebecca as the two left the Kings' kitchen to head for the food tables set outside near the barn. It had been Victor and Rebecca's turn to host worship services.

"Eli is a hard worker. I am happy to have him," Miriam went on.

Rebecca stopped walking. "You really mean it?" she asked, turning so she could look Miriam right in the eye.

Miriam nodded. "Of course. I had reservations at first. I admit it. But I was wrong to worry. Eli has worked out very well. And his leg seems to be healing nicely. He favors it much less, I think."

"Yes." Rebecca nodded. "He does. He walks almost all the way home now, which is a help to Victor. It was difficult, always having to pick Eli up. The days are already so long. But Eli cannot drive again until Bishop John and the elders give their permission."

"I see," Miriam said.

The two women continued walking toward where the food tables were set up near the barn.

"I am relieved to hear you speak well of Eli," Rebecca continued after a moment. "It matches what I feel myself. I was very uncertain when Victor first proposed he come to live with us. I know Victor hoped his influence would be a help to Eli, but I worried what Eli's influence would be on our own little ones."

"But it's turned out better than you hoped," Miriam filled in.

"It has." Rebecca nodded. "He's very good with the little ones, in fact, and I think he's even more stern with the older ones than Victor is sometimes. It's as if Eli doesn't want them to repeat his mistakes."

"That certainly doesn't sound wild," Miriam said.

"It doesn't, does it?" Rebecca agreed, her voice thoughtful.

"Mamm!" a high-pitched voice suddenly cried. A young girl in a dark dress and sky blue apron came hurtling toward them.

"Oh, my," Rebecca said, and Miriam could hear both humor and exasperation running through the other woman's voice. "I wonder what the crisis is this time."

"Give me the cookies," Miriam suggested. She shifted the larger plate she held so that she could balance a second, lighter one. "I can manage."

"If you're sure," Rebecca said.

"Positive." Miriam nodded. She took the plate, then watched Rebecca hurry toward her young daughter. The girl seized her mother by the hand, talking a mile a minute, and began to tug her back the way she had come. They disappeared around the side of the house. Smiling to herself, Miriam continued on toward the barn.

I'm glad I'm not the only one to notice Eli's hard work, she thought as she walked along. Perhaps she and Rebecca could put in a good word with Bishop John. Though the day when she would close the farm stand for the winter was still far off, Miriam wondered suddenly what would happen to Eli at the end of the harvest. Would he stay in his brother's house or go back to Ohio?

"You notice *she* didn't come today," a voice suddenly said, slicing across her thoughts.

Miriam stopped short. Not a half dozen steps in front of her was the corner of the barn. Turn that corner, and she would be at the food tables, where many of the other women were already gathered, setting out the food that was always a part of the social time after the worship service was over.

I know that voice, Miriam thought. She was almost certain it was Berthe Meyer, the woman Sarah had once been so afraid Daed would marry that her fear had kept her up at night.

"Of course she didn't," a second voice said. "She hasn't come once all summer, I notice. But then, why would she? She left the community, after all. She was never baptized."

And that's Erma, Miriam thought. Erma, Berthe's oldest

183

daughter, was not much older than Miriam. She had married Stephen Fisher the year before Daniel and Miriam were married. Miriam had never really liked Erma Meyer when they were growing up, though she had never admitted this to anyone, not even Sarah.

"I still think it's funny that Jacob would just let her go off like that," Erma went on. "I heard he even gave her his blessing! Can you believe that? He didn't even try to change her mind!"

"Things would have been much different if those girls had had a mother," Berthe Meyer huffed. "A man on his own raising two girls like that. Anyone could see nothing good would come of it."

"But surely something did," a new voice put in, one Miriam did not recognize. "Miriam and Daniel are a fine couple. Anyone can see that."

"A fine couple with no children," Berthe Meyer came back at once. "Anyone can see that as well. Though I will say this much: Much as I pity her, Miriam has backbone. Imagine, just the three of them in that house together, with everybody knowing the truth."

"What truth?" Miriam still couldn't identify the speaker, but she no longer cared.

"Why, that Daniel would have married the younger sister, Sarah, if he could." Erma spoke before even her mother could get a word in edgewise. "She was always making eyes at him when we were growing up. Then she up and left and Daniel married Miriam instead before the year was out. But she was never the one he really wanted. You mark my words. And still no children after all these years. That tells you something right there, doesn't it?"

"Poor Miriam," the unknown woman said. "I had no idea."

"Well, it's not really the sort of thing you talk about," Berthe Meyer said.

Miriam would have laughed aloud if only she could have caught her breath. But it seemed to her suddenly as if there was not enough air in all the world. Her lips parted. She panted for breath, but still she could not fill her lungs. Her whole body flushed. She trembled. Spots danced before her eyes. From fury or lack of oxygen she genuinely could not tell.

Away. I've got to get away, she thought. Away from the sniping and the false pity. Away before anyone knew what she had overheard. *That* she had overheard.

She turned, only vaguely aware that she was still clutching the plates of food in her hands. Her feet felt like lead as she lifted them to walk back across the yard. Finally, she sank down on the Kings' front steps, cradling the plates of food in her lap.

"Miriam?" As if from a great distance, she heard a voice speak her name. "Miriam!" A hand touched her shoulder, shaking gently, then with more insistence. "Miriam, are you all right?"

Slowly Miriam turned her head, focused her eyes. Leah Gingerich's concerned face swam into view.

"Leah," Miriam croaked out.

"Miriam, what is it?" Leah asked, and even through her strange haze Miriam could hear the fear and worry in the young woman's voice. "You're so white. Don't you feel well?"

"That's it. Yes, that's it," Miriam said, suddenly seizing on the possibility that Leah offered. "I don't feel well. I wonder, would you see if you can find Daniel for me? I think that I would like to go home."

"Of course I will," Leah said. After a moment's hesitation, Leah took the plates that Miriam had forgotten about from her lap and set them on the step beside her. "Do you want anything—some water, maybe—before I go?"

"No, *danki*, Leah," Miriam replied. "If you would just . . . *please*, Leah."

"I'm going," Leah said. Pivoting on one heel, she dashed off.

Miriam sat on the steps, hands folded tightly in her lap, and gazed straight ahead at nothing. If only, she thought, she could feel nothing as well.

Leah sped across the yard, skirting around the back side of the barn so that she'd attract less attention. She wasn't quite sure where Daniel was, but she was sure that the last thing Miriam needed was for Leah to go charging around calling attention to herself by searching for him. Then everyone would know that something bad had happened.

How dare those old biddies? Leah thought. She had been too far away to hear most of what had been said, but Leah had been at the perfect angle to see what had happened. The group of women clustered around the food tables, leaning in to listen as Berthe Meyer and her daughter spoke. And Miriam was about to come around the edge of the barn. Leah heard only a few words but it was clear that they were talking about Miriam and her marriage. Leah didn't want to hear any more; she had stopped short, then staggered away. Just the thought of the wounded expression in Miriam's eyes made Leah's own eyes fill with angry tears.

Oomph!

With a suddenness that left her gasping, Leah collided with another body. She staggered back and felt strong hands close around her arms, steadying her, holding her upright.

"Leah, what is it?" a voice asked urgently. "What's wrong?"

Leah looked up into Eli's forest green eyes.

"Eli," she sobbed out. "Oh, Eli."

"You're crying!" Eli exclaimed. He took a quick step back, studying her intently. "Leah, are you injured? *Tell me what's wrong.*"

"Not me," Leah gasped out. She reached to dash the angry tears from her cheeks. "It isn't me. It's—"

"Miriam," Eli said.

Leah's mouth dropped open. "How did you know?"

"Leah." Unexpectedly, her name came out on a sigh. "I'm not stupid, you know, and I'm certainly not blind. I know how much you look up to Miriam. If you're this upset, it has to be about somebody you really care about. I've just seen your *aenti* and *onkel*, so I know that they are well. That leaves Miriam, or you yourself, and you tell me you're fine. So, once again, we're back to Miriam."

"It was awful," Leah whispered. "Oh, Eli." To Leah's dismay and annoyance, she began to weep once more, huge

187

tears that welled up and rolled down her cheeks. Eli released her to fish in his back pocket for a handkerchief. Then, before Leah realized what he intended, he tilted up her chin and wiped the tears from her face, precisely as Aenti Rachel had always done when she was small. Then he tucked the handkerchief into Leah's hand.

"What was so awful?" he asked. "Tell me."

"The women at the food table," Leah blurted out. "I couldn't hear much of what they were saying. But I could see who was speaking. It was that horrible Berthe Meyer and her daughter Erma, who's just as bad. So I knew what it meant. They were gossiping."

"Gossiping about Miriam?" Eli asked.

Leah nodded. "I think so, yes, because I could see Miriam, too. She was carrying some plates of food for the table. She was about to come around the side of the barn. But when she heard the women speaking, she stopped, and then she turned around. They must have been saying something terrible. I could tell by the way she was walking that something was wrong. It was like she couldn't see what was right in front of her. For a minute, I was afraid she might fall down. And the look on her face . . . She says she wants to go home. She wants me to find Daniel. Have you seen him?"

"No," Eli said, turning quickly to look behind him. "Come, let's look for him."

They set off at a quick walk, moving through the crowd of people gathering for the meal.

"I don't see him by the food tables," Eli said. "But there are still more people coming out of the barn. Let's head that way."

"I don't understand it," Leah said, still furious on Miriam's behalf. "Why do people do things like that? Don't they stop to think about how it might make other people feel?"

"No," Eli said. "They do not. People who gossip think only of themselves."

Leah opened her mouth to ask how on earth he would know such a thing, then closed it with a snap. *Of course he knows,* she realized. She now understood why Eli assumed she had heard the gossip about him.

"I'm sorry," she said. "It must be terrible to know that people are talking about you behind your back, and there's nothing you can do to stop it."

Some quick emotion flashed across Eli's face, there and gone so swiftly Leah had no chance of identifying it.

"It is, in fact," he said. "But you get used to it."

"I don't think that can be right," Leah said. She pulled in a deep breath. "I want you to know that I never told anyone what you told me when we were driving back from town the other day. I never talked about you behind your back. And I know that I have faults, lots and lots of them. But I would not do that—not to you or anyone. And I understand now what you were trying to say about that *Englischer* boy in that red car. You were trying to tell me to be careful or people might be gossiping about me. I guess I should say thank you for that."

"You say the most amazing things sometimes," Eli said. "Though I think the most amazing thing of all is that I followed all of that. I—"

"Eli! Where have you got to? I need your help." Victor's voice rang out.

Eli's head whipped in the direction of his brother's voice.

"I'm here," he called back. "I'll be right there." He turned to Leah once more. "It looks as if the men are still in the barn. I bet I can find Daniel there. I am sure Victor has seen him."

"*Danki*, Eli," Leah said. "I will go back to Miriam."

But as Leah headed back toward the house, she saw that things were not as she'd left them. Miriam was no longer on the steps of the King house but sitting on a bench on one end of the porch. And Leah's *aenti* was climbing the steps of the porch, heading straight for Miriam.

Thank goodness! Aenti Rachel could make anyone feel better, Leah thought as she turned back around and continued her search for Daniel.

Thirteen

Oh, Miriam," Rachel said. "There you are."

Miriam started. She was feeling a little better, well enough that she realized the surest way to head off any additional gossip about her was to stop sitting out in plain sight on the front steps of Victor and Rebecca's porch. She had pushed herself up, collecting the plates of food as she stood. For one brief moment, Miriam had considered turning around. Marching down the steps and around the side of the barn to confront Berthe Meyer and the others. To see their faces when they realized she knew what they had said.

It's what Sarah would have done, she thought. But Miriam was not Sarah. She could never be Sarah, and wasn't that the problem? In the end, she had simply walked to a bench at the far end of the porch, sinking down upon it and setting the plates of food at her side. Then she'd sat perfectly still, her mind as blank as a new sheet of paper, until she'd heard the sound of someone saying her name.

Miriam looked up. Slowly, as if she had to regain the use of her eyes, a familiar face came into focus.

"Rachel?" Miriam asked, her voice coming out in a croak.

"I saw you sitting here on your own," Rachel said in a calm, straightforward tone. "I thought you might like some company."

"Danke," Miriam said. She hadn't wanted to talk to anyone. But Rachel was the exception. Rachel's company was always welcome. "I wasn't feeling well and wanted to go home early," Miriam explained. "I'm just waiting here for Daniel."

Rachel made a face. "He's involved in a spirited discussion about the upcoming horse auction, I'm afraid."

"Oh, well, in that case," Miriam said. She cleared her throat, striving to match Rachel's easy manner. "We might as well get comfortable. We'll be here a while."

Rachel's kind eyes sharpened in concern. "But are you all right?"

"It's nothing serious. My stomach is upset." This was not far from the truth, Miriam told herself. "I just came to sit here, because I don't think I can eat the meal. Don't worry. Leah said she would look for Daniel for me."

"I'm sure Daniel will come once he knows you need him," Rachel said.

Miriam made an inarticulate sound. She lifted a hand to her mouth, pressing hard against it to keep from sobbing aloud. Rachel sat beside her in silence, eyes straight ahead,

hands folded quietly in her lap. Never had Miriam appreci-
ated the other woman more. One touch, one word, even a
single syllable of support, and Miriam was sure she would
have lost control. She pulled in deep breaths, focusing on
the air moving in and out of her lungs. After a few moments, she dropped her hand down into her lap. She swallowed hard.

"Did I ever tell you," Rachel said after several minutes
had passed, her tone conversational, as if she were discussing the weather or the garden, "that, at one time in my life,
I thought I might become your mother?"

Miriam's head turned toward Rachel as if jerked by a
string, all thoughts of her present upset forgotten.

"What?"

Rachel smiled. And now she did reach for Miriam's
hands, giving them a quick squeeze before releasing them
to fold her own in her lap once more.

"Of course, it was many years ago, about a year after
Edna died. Jacob's first year of mourning had come to an
end and everybody just assumed he would begin looking
for another wife. It wasn't so unreasonable. That would
have been the sensible, Plain thing to do, after all. He had
two young girls to raise, and he was just a little over thirty,
still a vital man. Surely he would want more children; he
would want a more traditional family life.

"I'm still not quite sure how it happened," Rachel continued quietly, "but the day came when I suddenly realized
that everyone around me seemed to be of the opinion that *I*
would be Jacob's choice."

The two women sat in silence for several moments, Miriam waiting for Rachel to continue. How many more surprises could the day hold?

"Did they say why?" she finally managed to inquire.

At this, Rachel gave a quick laugh. "Oh, yes. Over and over," she replied. "Though never to my face, of course. But I'm sure you don't need me to tell you how effective gossip can be."

"No, I don't," Miriam agreed.

"I was considered old to still be unmarried," Rachel went on. "Just a little over twenty. Apparently, a marriage between Jacob and me would be the perfect solution to both our 'problems.' He would get a mother for his children, and I would be spared becoming an old maid.

"Everyone around me seemed so sure of what would happen that, eventually, I became sure of it myself. I even became convinced that this was what I wanted: I wanted to become Jacob Lapp's wife."

"Daed never spoke about any of this," Miriam said.

"I don't imagine that he did," Rachel answered with a smile. "But then, he had no reason to, did he? He had made his choice, and I'm sure he never regretted it."

"The choice not to marry you, you mean?" Miriam asked.

"The choice not to marry anyone," Rachel corrected her softly. She fell silent for a moment. Her eyes looked straight ahead, but it seemed to Miriam that Rachel was no longer seeing what was right in front of her, the Kings' front porch. Instead, she was seeing something that had happened many years ago.

Rachel finally spoke once more. "I still remember the

Sunday Jacob asked if he could speak with me after worship service. I was so excited! So sure that this was the day he would ask me to become his wife. I had butterflies in my stomach all during the service. I don't think I heard a word the bishop spoke. All I could do was try to picture the moment when Jacob would ask me to be his wife.

"After the service, we went for a ride in his buggy. We drove to the top of Stoneridge Hill. Do you know the place I mean?"

"I do." Miriam nodded. It was a popular courting spot. "It's beautiful there. You can see in every direction."

"In every direction," Rachel echoed. "As if the whole world could be yours." She paused yet again, as if she could see the view before her, right at that very moment. "We got out of the buggy," Rachel continued. "Jacob even held my hand. His touch was strong and steady. I remember that so well! Just as I remember the quiet, steady way his eyes held mine when he told me how sorry he was that he could not ask me to be his wife. It wasn't me, he said. I shouldn't think that it was. But he would never marry anyone."

"But *why*?" Miriam said. "Why would he be so opposed to taking another wife?"

"For the simplest reason imaginable," Rachel answered. "Because in his heart, he still had one. Your father was, and always would be, married to your mother. Nothing was ever going to change that, he said. Not even the fact that Edna wasn't alive anymore, that now she walked with God. Believing that, *knowing* that, the way he did, he could never ask another woman to become his wife."

Rachel gave a long, deep sigh. Looking into the other

woman's face, Miriam discovered there were tears in Rachel's eyes.

"Your father loved your mother, Miriam. I have never seen a love quite like it, not in all my life. Another man might have done what everyone expected of him, and it certainly would have made life easier. He would have had a helpmate, someone to help him raise you and Sarah, to run the house, the farm stand, and the farm.

"But Jacob Lapp was not that man. He knew his own heart and mind. Even more, he believed that he could not feel as strongly, see as clearly, as he did, if the path he was choosing to walk was not also the will of God. And this faith gave him the strength to choose a path that many people would not understand, might even criticize him for."

"Sarah," Miriam whispered. Sarah had sounded so much like Daed that day in the blackberry patch. Sarah, too, had followed a rocky path, but it was the one she believed God had paved for her inside her heart.

"I have always thought that Sarah and your father were much alike," Rachel said. "But you are like him, also. You have his steadiness and his quiet determination. You have the same devotion to those you love."

"But what if they don't love you back?" Miriam whispered, and she felt a fine trembling seize all her limbs. This was as close as she had ever come to speaking of her innermost fears to anyone.

"What I think," Rachel answered slowly, "what I learned from Jacob that day, is that we can never know what is in another person's heart. Not until they decide to share it with us. Until that moment, we have only our own hopes and perhaps our fears."

Unexpectedly, she smiled once more. "We certainly have our own expectations, which may or may not be met! As long as I'm telling you the truth, I must also say that I didn't take what your father had to say particularly well. I was upset. I was *very* upset. I felt that I'd been made to look like a fool, and that it was all Jacob's fault.

"But as the days passed and I had the chance to think about all he said to me that day, I changed my mind. The more I thought about it, the more I could see how courageous Jacob was. How honorable, even, to explain to me why he could not marry me, rather than to simply leave me dangling, never knowing the truth. Or marrying me, knowing I would speak the vows in good faith, but for him, they would have been false.

"And, slowly but surely, I realized something else: Jacob's actions had created in me the desire to look beyond what others thought I should do. His courage gave me the courage to look into, and to know, what was in my own heart.

"John Miller and I were married that winter. He's younger than I am by several years, you know. People flapped their lips about that, too, but I never let it bother me. I knew, just as Jacob did, that I had made the right choice."

Miriam was silent, taking in Rachel's words, taking in all the unspoken things she thought the older woman was trying to tell her.

"I cannot be sorry that Daed made the choice he did,"

she said at last. "Because then, I think, I would have to be sorry that he was who he was. But I think having you for a mother would have been a fine thing, for Sarah and for me."

"I will tell you a secret," Rachel said. "In my heart, I have always thought of you as my daughters. And I have always been proud of you both."

"Oh, Rachel," Miriam sobbed.

"There, now!" Rachel said. She put an arm around Miriam's shoulders. "I tried to make you feel better, but still you are crying after all."

"You have made me feel better," Miriam said. "More than you know. And I don't know what's come over me lately." She scrubbed away the tears with the backs of her hands. "It seems I'm crying all the time."

"You have had many changes in the last few months, Miriam," Rachel said. "Sometimes, getting used to them takes time. It is hard to be patient, particularly with ourselves. Ah! And here is Daniel, just in time."

Rachel gave Miriam's shoulder one final pat, and then stood up. "Here we are, Daniel," she called out.

"Miriam," Daniel said. He strode toward them. Even from a distance, Miriam could hear the worry in her husband's voice. "Is everything all right? Eli said you were feeling unwell."

"Eli!" Miriam exclaimed.

"Leah must have asked him to speak to Daniel," Rachel said. "So that she would not call attention to herself, and him, by asking to speak to him when there were so many menfolk around." She took a step away from the bench where Miriam still sat. "Well, I will leave you two alone.

But I will call on you tomorrow to see how you get on, Miriam. Good day to you, Daniel."

"Good day, Rachel," Daniel said. The second she was past him, he knelt at Miriam's feet, gazing intently into her face. "You look pale," he said. "Let me take you home."

"I would like to go home," Miriam admitted. "But I hate to have you leave, Daniel. This will be your last chance to talk with all the other men before the horse auction."

"I'll take my chances with the auction," Daniel said. "If you are unwell—"

"It's nothing really," Miriam assured him, "and it will not be a problem for me to take the buggy on my own. That is, if you don't mind walking."

"Of course I don't," Daniel said at once. "Or, if there is room, I can ride home with my mother and father." He looked at her again, concern in his blue eyes. "You're sure?"

"Yes, I am sure," Miriam told him.

"Very well. Then I'll just go get the horse hitched up. Do you want to wait here, or will you come?"

"I'll wait here," Miriam said.

She expected Daniel to get up at once, but, to her surprise, he stayed right where he was. With gentle fingers, he reached out and touched Miriam's cheek. "I think, perhaps, you look a little better."

"Anything would be an improvement, don't you think?" Miriam said, striving to keep her tone light. Her skin tingled everywhere Daniel's fingers had touched her.

Daniel smiled. "A sensible man would refuse to answer that," he said. "And I *am* sensible. Even my mother says so. Wait there. I'll be right back."

He rose, turned, and sprinted down the porch steps, heading for the barn. Abruptly Miriam realized that, against all odds, she was smiling.

Twenty minutes later she brought the horse and buggy to a halt just outside the graveyard. She looped the reins around the stock, and then climbed down from the buggy, giving the horse a pat on the nose as she walked by him. "I'll only be a moment," she promised in a quiet voice. Then she was threading her way among the graves, making for the place where her mother and father were buried side by side.

Miriam had not visited this place since the day her father was buried, only a month earlier. The earth above her father's resting place was now smooth and green, though the grass was not yet as long as on her mother's grave. Miriam hesitated for a moment, suddenly uncertain, and then sat down at the place where the two graves met.

"Oh, Daed," she whispered. "I wish that I had known."

Known how great, how extraordinary, was her father's love for her mother. So great that not even death could erase it from his heart. How had Rachel described Jacob Lapp? Quiet, steady, determined. And she had said Miriam was just like that.

A late afternoon breeze ruffled the grass on top of the graves. Miriam felt it frisking about her face, lifting the strings of her *kapp*. Miriam felt her heart lift along with the breeze.

I did know, she realized. She had felt her father's love for her mother every day of her life. Jacob's love for Edna Lapp had been inseparable from who he was. He had said as much to Rachel. Because he was courageous, Miriam thought. Brave enough to understand, and to embrace, the innermost workings of his own heart.

Help me, Daed, she thought. *Help me to be more than simply quiet and steady. Help me to be as brave as you were, all the days of my life.*

Brave enough to acknowledge her hopes and fears. And brave enough to live with whatever might come when she finally found the courage to speak them aloud.

Fourteen

Miriam came awake slowly. Late afternoon sunlight streamed in through the bedroom window, spilling across the honey-colored floors, filling the room with a warm, luxurious glow. Miriam lay still, her head on her own pillow, one hand, palm upward, resting on the pillow where Daniel's head would be when he lay down beside her.

Even in sleep, she thought, *I reach for Daniel, my love, my husband.*

She waited for the familiar pang of pain and uncertainty that thinking about how much she loved Daniel usually brought her. But it didn't come. Miriam wiggled her fingers, just to make sure she was really awake. Perhaps she was still dreaming, she thought. But her sleep had been without dreams. Her sleep had been quiet and calm, exactly as she felt right this moment. Peaceful, like a ship that had been battling a storm at sea for a very long time but had now, finally, made its way safely home to port.

What has happened? she wondered.

It wasn't as if she had done anything momentous. She'd just taken a nap. That was all. It hadn't been until Miriam had put the horse and buggy away, giving the horse some oats to munch on before coming into the house, that she had realized just how tired she was. She had climbed the stairs to the bedroom, intending merely to change out of her good dress and apron before going back down. Supper would be a cold one and was already prepared, as was always the case on Sunday.

But the bed looked so inviting! Miriam's whole body felt heavy, as if every cell were crying out for her to lie down. Giving in to impulse, she had changed into her everyday dress, but left off her apron and removed her *kapp*, setting it on her dressing table. Then, finally, she had simply given in and curled up on top of the quilt. She'd pulled the knitted afghan that was always draped over the end of the bed up over her legs and feet, closed her eyes, and remembered nothing more.

Miriam pushed herself upright slowly, sitting propped up against the headboard. She could see out the window now and look out across the fields, shorn of their hay, the great, round bales curing in the sun. Miriam inhaled deeply. The rich, green smell, which seemed to be the smell of the very earth itself, filled her nostrils.

I have so much to be thankful for, she thought. She loved this farm that was, and had always been, her home. She couldn't imagine ever wanting to leave it, as Sarah had done.

Again, Miriam waited for the pang that so often followed swiftly upon any thought of her sister, and again, there was none. Miriam sat very still. Then, once more obeying an impulse she could not explain but that would not be denied, she reached out and slid the Bible that always rested on the nightstand into her lap. She held it for a moment, then, abruptly, she released it, letting the pages fall open of their own accord. Only then did Miriam look down.

"'Clothe yourselves with humility toward one another,'" she read, "'for God is opposed to the proud, but gives grace to the humble. Therefore humble yourselves under the mighty hand of God that He may exalt you at the proper time, casting all your anxiety on Him, because He cares for you . . . After you have suffered for a little while, the God of all grace, who called you to His eternal glory in Christ, will Himself perfect, confirm, strengthen, and establish you.'"

Miriam leaned her head back and closed her eyes. *I do feel stronger,* she thought. *And I have Daed to thank for it.* It was her father who had helped her to see what must be done, the path that she must follow, just as he had done when he was alive.

I have not been humble, Miriam thought as she opened her eyes. Instead, she had been proud, insisting that the only position for her in Daniel's heart must be the first one, because that was the place Daniel held in Miriam's own heart.

But how fortunate she was! Daniel was her husband. Every day, Miriam could awaken to the fact that Daniel had chosen *her*, not any of the other women in their community. He had asked Miriam to be his wife. His face was the first thing she saw each morning, the last thing she saw at night. Each and every day, Miriam could see and touch the man she loved. She could listen for the tread of his feet upon the stairs and the sound of his voice.

Daed loved Mamm in the same way that I love Daniel, Miriam thought. But her parents had not been so fortunate. Edna had died when they were both so young. But her father's love had never wavered. It had not died. It had stayed alive and strong. In all the years from the day of his wife's death to the day of his own, Jacob's love had burned, quiet and steady, inside his heart, a heart made courageous by the grace of God.

Miriam closed the Bible gently and returned it to the nightstand. Then she slid from the bed to kneel by its side.

Great and merciful God, she prayed as she bowed her head, *I thank You for Your guidance. I thank You for opening my eyes. Help my heart find the courage to walk the path You have prepared for me. Let me walk it with humility, being truly grateful for the gifts that You bestow.*

For several moments after the words of her prayer had ended, Miriam continued to kneel beside the bed. But it seemed to her in those moments that she was still praying, a prayer without conscious thought, her mind, her soul reaching up and out, reaching in every direction for the clear and glorious presence of God.

She got to her feet filled with the same sense of calm with which she had awoken. She was moving toward her dressing table to retrieve her *kapp* when a movement outside the window caught her eye. Miriam stepped to the window and looked out, and in that moment, it seemed to her as if she were transported back in time to that day six years earlier.

She could see Daniel and Sarah coming across the fields together. Daniel was speaking, gesturing with his arms for emphasis, as he had on that day so long ago. And just like on that day, Sarah stopped him with a touch, the simple gesture of laying a hand upon his arm. For what seemed to Miriam like endless moments, her sister and husband faced each other. Then Sarah reached up and threw her arms around Daniel's neck. Daniel pulled Sarah to him, burying his face in the crook of her shoulder.

Miriam never knew how long they stood that way. She turned her back on the window and walked to her dressing table. She lifted her *kapp* and settled it over her hair. Then she tied on her favorite everyday apron, the one whose color always reminded her of the roses in the garden.

She paused and gazed at her reflection in the mirror. A young woman, her expression serious and her gaze steady, looked back.

This is who I am, she thought. It was time to prove she was her father's daughter. Time to prove that she had the courage and conviction of what lay in her own heart.

On silent feet, Miriam walked down the stairs to do what her heart knew must be done.

Fifteen

"Miriam, you should have waited for me to do that," Sarah exclaimed as she came into the kitchen. Not even ten minutes had passed since Miriam watched Sarah throw her arms around Daniel's neck.

As she had throughout their childhood, Sarah thrust a leg backward to catch the screen door so that it wouldn't slam behind her. "I keep telling you that I can help." She moved to stand beside Miriam as she was laying the table for supper and placed a hand on her arm. "Are you feeling all right? I met Daniel walking across the fields. He said you came home early because you weren't feeling well."

"I wasn't," Miriam said. "But I'm much better now." She set the last knife down on the table, adjusting it so that it was perfectly straight. Then she turned to face her sister.

"I know you and Daniel walked home together," she said quietly. "I saw you from the window upstairs."

Sarah's brow furrowed. "What?"

"I saw you, Sarah," Miriam said again. "Just like I saw you that summer, before you left, before Daniel and I were married. And I want you to know . . ." Her voice wavered, and Miriam broke off. She took a deep, steadying breath, and then went on, "I want you to know that I understand and it's all right."

The furrow between Sarah's brows became an out-and-out frown. "Understand what, Miriam? What are you talking about?"

"I'm talking about the fact that you and Daniel are in love."

Sarah's face turned the color of ashes. Her hand slipped from Miriam's arm. "What?" she whispered. "What did you just say?"

"I know that Daniel loves you best, Sarah," Miriam answered as steadily as she could. "And—" She felt her heart breaking, but she forced herself to finish. "And that he only married me because he couldn't have you."

There was something about the expression in Sarah's eyes that Miriam couldn't read. Miriam had thought that Sarah would be relieved to know that Miriam knew the truth and that she didn't blame Sarah or Daniel—that she didn't mind. Instead, Sarah looked as if Miriam had stabbed her through the heart.

"I—I've known it since the day you told Daed and me that you were going away," Miriam faltered on. "I just . . . hid from it, I guess. But I don't want to hide anymore."

"But everything you know is wrong!" Sarah said. "How can you think such a thing, Miriam? How can you have lived with Daniel all this time and not know?"

"Not know what?"

"That he loves *you*!" Sarah cried. "He's loved you ever since the day he tumbled over and almost squashed you flat when you were, what—two years old!"

"Three," Miriam answered faintly. "It's Daniel who was two."

Sarah groped blindly for the chair behind her, then slowly sank down. "Oh, my stars. That's how long *you've* loved *him*, isn't it? Since that same day. Since you were three years old."

And then, to Miriam's complete and utter astonishment, Sarah began to laugh.

Miriam reached to take her sister by the shoulders, shaking her furiously. "Stop laughing at me. Stop it right now!"

"I'm not laughing at you," Sarah said. "Really. It's just all so . . . crazy." She stood up, pushing Miriam's hands away from her shoulders. "I mean it, Miriam. *You* stop now. Stop listening to whatever stories you've been telling yourself and listen to me.

"Daniel loves *you*. He has always loved you."

"You can't know that. How can you know that?" Miriam whispered.

"Well, how do you think?" Sarah demanded. "Because he told me so. In fact, he has been telling me so, quite relentlessly, since he was thirteen."

"But I saw you!" Miriam cried. "I saw you and Daniel

together, this afternoon . . . just like six years ago. I saw the way the two of you embraced, Sarah. Don't try and tell me you don't care for each other."

"I'm not trying to tell you that," Sarah said, in a steady, even tone. "We do care, very much. But that's not the same as saying we're in love. We're not. We never have been, Miriam. I don't know why you would ever think we were."

"Because it's what everyone else thought!" Miriam said. "Do you hear me? Everyone! It was all I heard, after every Sunday worship service, at every quilt frolic when I left the room and people thought I couldn't hear what they said while I was gone. What a lovely couple Daniel and Sarah make. How alike they are."

"Which only goes to show that people are idiots," Sarah answered with a snort. "Daniel and I are no more alike than—" She made a face as she searched for the proper combination. "Oh, I don't know!" she finally exclaimed. "Pineapples and bunny rabbits."

"That's a ridiculous comparison," Miriam protested.

"I know that!" Sarah said. "I'm thinking that would be the point."

"Stop trying to sound like an *Englischer*," Miriam snapped.

"*I* am *an Englischer!*" Sarah came right back. "Or as good as, anyhow. And just because you're Plain doesn't mean you're not trying to change the subject. Daniel and I were *arguing* when you saw us. Actually, both times."

Miriam shook her head. "You were arguing with Daniel? What could you two possibly have to argue about?"

"I just told you," Sarah said with exaggerated patience.

"You. *You* are the only subject we've ever talked about. All his life, Daniel has been so in love with you, and so afraid that you didn't love him back. He has never known how to tell you.

"Long before I told Daed that I wanted to go away to school, Daniel decided that he wanted to marry you. But he didn't know how to tell you, how to make you fall in love with him. He was sure you didn't care for him at all."

"But how could that be?" Miriam asked, astounded. "I'd loved Daniel all my life."

Sarah gave her sister a long, exasperated look. "I don't think either one of you is very good at saying the things that matter most. Or at least, not the things that are closest to your heart."

"Perhaps that's true," Miriam admitted. And there was something else that was true: She had been pulling away from Daniel then, convinced that he loved Sarah.

"Anyway," Sarah said, "Daniel was in a panic about how to court you. What should he say, how should he say it, when and where should he ask you? I tried to help him as best I could, but I had other concerns. I was trying to understand what I was meant to do with my own life, and once it was clear, I had to act on it before I lost my courage.

"So I meant to wait with my announcement until after Daniel announced his intentions, but that day with Daed, it just came out of me. It was such a huge decision for me, I couldn't keep it bottled up inside."

"I can understand that," Miriam said. "But I still don't understand why you and Daniel argued."

"Because he was furious with me," Sarah told her. "I think

he was counting on me to guide his every step until you were actually married, and instead I left." She sighed. "I admit, I became impatient with Daniel. The day that we argued, I told him that if he wanted to marry you, then he had to learn to stand on his own two feet and make his feelings known." Sarah winced. "I told him he had to be man enough to figure this out on his own or he wouldn't be worthy of you."

Miriam was silent as she took all that in. Was it really possible that Daniel had turned to Sarah—as a kind of adviser—because he was terrified he might not be able to win Miriam on his own? It was possible, she supposed. Daniel had never been one to discuss his feelings or emotions. Still, she had to ask . . .

"But what about when you hugged each other?"

Sarah smiled. "After I scolded him, Daniel came to his senses. He admitted that I was right. Then he apologized and he asked if we could still be friends. I told him we were more than friends, that I'd always thought of him as a brother, and once you two married, we'd be family. That's when we hugged."

"And today?" Miriam asked faintly.

"Men are so dense sometimes!" Sarah exclaimed. "I met him walking along the road, and he said you had come home early because you didn't feel well. When I asked what the matter was he said he didn't know! He'd just let you come home, alone, while he stayed behind to talk to the men about the horse auction. Of course, he told me that you'd insisted you could go on your own, just the way you insist on never letting anyone help with the housework. It obviously never occurred to him that you might really be unwell—or unhappy. I was very blunt. I told him: "How can Miriam know how much you love her if you never put her first?" He was angry at me, but then he was grateful. So he hugged me—like the brother he has always been to me."

Now it was Miriam who sat down. She put her elbows on the table and rested her head in her hands. "I don't understand anything anymore," she said. "This is not what I expected to hear from you."

"Now, *that* I believe," Sarah said. She sat down, too. The two sisters sat in silence for several moments.

"You really married Daniel believing he loved me more than he loved you?" Sarah finally spoke. "Miriam, how could you do such a thing? How could you live like that?"

"Because of how much I loved him," Miriam said into her hands. She lifted her head. "I know you were only joking, but what you said was true. I really have loved Daniel since I was three years old and he was two."

"And have you mentioned this to him?" Sarah asked.

"Probably not," Miriam said.

"That's not good enough, Miriam," Sarah said. "Have you told Daniel that you love him, *ja* or no?"

"No," Miriam whispered as her eyes filled with tears. "Not right out. Not like that. I thought . . . I suppose I thought that I would show him somehow. Isn't that the Plain way? You know, the way Daed showed us he loved us all those years. He never made flowery speeches."

"No," Sarah agreed. "He did not. But he told us that he loved us every single day, when he tucked us into bed each night. Surely you can't have forgotten that."

"No," Miriam said, "I have not."

"So why would you never tell Daniel that you loved him?"

"Because I knew that he never loved me," Miriam cried. "He loved you!"

"No," Sarah said. She reached across the table to take Miriam's hands in hers. "You have to believe me, Miriam. Daniel has spent his entire life loving *you*—you and only you. I was like a sister to him, the person who knew you better than anyone else. That's why he talked to me. *So he could find a way to spend his life with you.* If I'd known what you thought—"

"What am I going to do?" Miriam whispered. "Oh, Sarah, I've been so wrong."

"You don't need me to tell you the answer to that," Sarah said. "You know perfectly well yourself."

Miriam pulled in a deep breath, then let it out again. "I'm going to have to be brave again, aren't I?"

"You are brave," Sarah said. "You're the bravest person I know. And I'll tell you a secret." All of a sudden, she grinned. "Right before I came in, I think Daniel said something about heading to the barn to check on the horse."

"Check on the horse!" Miriam exclaimed as she got to her feet. "What's he going to do that for? As if I don't know how to care for a horse and buggy after all these years. Any good Plain woman knows that."

"Any good Plain wife," Sarah corrected her, her eyes dancing. "Clearly, there are all sorts of things you need to remind Daniel of."

Miriam laughed, then clapped a hand across her mouth at the unexpected sound. "I laughed," she said, her tone full of wonder. "When I came home this afternoon, the last thing I expected was that I would find something to laugh about." She looked at her sister. "Thank you."

"Don't thank me," Sarah said. "Thank yourself."

"The—barn?" Miriam asked.

"The barn." Sarah nodded. "I'll just finish setting the table, if I may."

"You may," Miriam said.

She turned toward the door. The few short steps it took from the table to the steps were the longest Miriam had ever taken. But finally, she was down the steps and into the yard. She could see Daniel, standing beside the pump, his back to the house, gazing in the direction of the fields Miriam saw from her kitchen window each morning.

Is this what we've been doing all these years? she suddenly thought. *Looking at the same thing, for the same thing, but never knowing the other was looking as well?*

As she got closer, she saw that Daniel's hair was dripping wet. The front of his shirt and half the back were soaked, as if he'd simply thrust his head and shoulders beneath the spigot and worked the pump handle for all he was worth, never caring for an instant where the water would go. It was the first time in all their life together that such a thing had happened.

Miriam caught her breath. Just for a moment, her footsteps faltered. But she squared her shoulders and continued on to Daniel's side. He continued to stand, perfectly still.

"How much did you hear of my talk with Sarah?" Miriam asked quietly.

"Enough," Daniel answered after a moment. "Enough to know what a fool I've been."

"No more foolish than I," Miriam replied.

Daniel gave a short, harsh bark of laughter. "I don't know how you feel, but I think perhaps it takes more than that to make a good marriage."

"I will tell you how I feel, Daniel Brennemann," Miriam began.

At the sound of his full name, Daniel abruptly swung toward her. He reached for Miriam, seizing her tightly by the shoulders, cutting off her flow of words.

"No," he said fiercely. "I will speak first. I *must*."

Miriam stood perfectly still within Daniel's grasp, looking straight up into his eyes. At this moment, his eyes were no longer the same shade as the sky. For the sky above their heads was beginning to darken, making its way toward night. Against it, Daniel's eyes blazed out like piercing stars.

Miriam reached up and laid a hand against her husband's cheek, saw the way his eyes lit with surprise. Saw something she realized she had not seen there in a very long time, perhaps not even since the first days of their marriage. Hope.

"Daniel Brennemann," she said once more, "are we by any chance arguing about which of us gets to be the first to say *I love you*?"

Daniel let go of Miriam's shoulders so that he could place one hand atop her own. He turned his face to her hand and pressed a kiss into the very center of her palm. Miriam's whole body flushed with the heat of that kiss. It seemed to her that she could feel it making a circuit of all her limbs, finally coming to rest in the place she knew she would carry it forever: her heart, now almost whole. She made a wordless sound.

"I love you, Miriam," Daniel said. "I love you so much. There are days when it seems to me that I have loved you all my life. That I cannot tell where you end and I begin, I have loved you for so long. Perhaps that is why—"

"Hush," Miriam said as she reached with her other hand to cover Daniel's mouth. "I will not hear you reproach yourself. I have been selfish, Daniel. And I have been blind, so blind. I kept thinking you did not say you loved me because you *could* not. That I knew you well enough to know that you would never tell a lie. Not once did I stop to realize that I had never spoken the words myself. So, please, listen to me now.

"I love you. I have always loved you. I will love you 'til the day I die."

"Miriam," Daniel whispered. *"Miriam."*

He pulled her close and pressed his lips to hers. Miriam felt her heart rise up inside her chest, then slowly, gently come to rest, now whole. There was no part of it that harbored any fear or doubt. No part that was not filled with love. Love given and love received.

The kiss ended and Daniel held Miriam tightly.

"Daniel," Miriam murmured.

"No," Daniel said softly. He lifted her face up to his and kissed her once more, letting his lips roam across her face. "Not yet. I am not ready to return to the everyday world quite yet."

"I will tell you a secret, if you will let me," Miriam said.

She felt Daniel's laughter move through his body a second before it sounded. "Oh, you will, will you?" he asked. "And what is that?"

"This is the everyday world," Miriam said.

Daniel moved so quickly Miriam never even guessed his intention, pulling her even closer, holding her so tight and fast that it seemed to Miriam that they now truly embodied the words that he had spoken. She could not tell where she ended and he began.

"I love you. I love you," Daniel said. "It is you, and only you, that I've loved all my life. I will never forget to tell you again."

"And neither will I," Miriam said. "You're going to get tired of it, I'll say it so much. Only, Daniel . . ."

"What?" Daniel said.

"You're all wet."

Daniel gave a great shout of astonished laughter. So loud and joyous Miriam was sure it could be heard all over the county. And she was certain it had been heard by the great and merciful God who had finally showed the two of them the path that they should walk, and that it was one they would walk together.

"So I am," Daniel said. "And I'm making you wet, also. Come, let's go in. We can go upstairs and change." His eyes gazed down into Miriam's. "I don't know about you," he said softly, "but all of a sudden, I am very hungry."

At the heat in her husband's tone, Miriam flushed. But she kept her gaze just as steady as his.

"So am I."

"I could get used to this," Daniel said, a laugh in his voice. "Suddenly we agree about everything."

Miriam gave him a shove. Daniel reached for her, sneaking a quick kiss. Together they turned in the direction of the house.

"What is that?" Daniel asked suddenly. He lifted his head, literally scenting the air. "Do you smell that?"

Miriam breathed in deeply. "I do," she said. "It smells like fire."

"Miriam! Daniel!" she heard a voice cry out. As one, Miriam and Daniel turned in the direction of the voice. It was Lucas. He had come across the fields from the Brennemann farmhouse at a full run.

"The farm stand," he gasped. He bent, resting his hands on his knees as he struggled to catch his breath. "The farm stand is on fire."

Sixteen

W e can rebuild," Daniel said.

Miriam nodded, feeling dazed. Was it really still Sunday? So many things had happened that the morning seemed like a lifetime ago. She could barely believe that only a few short hours had passed since Lucas had come running to bring them the news of the fire.

The living room of the Lapp farmhouse was now crowded. Miriam and Sarah sat together on the couch, with Daniel perched on the arm at Miriam's side. The Millers were there, including Leah, as were all of Daniel's family except for Annaliese, who had taken the youngest children home to bed. The *Englisch* firefighters had just departed. When Daniel had expressed the family's solemn thanks, the captain had shared his regret that he and his crew hadn't been able to do more. The old farm stand had burned fast and hot.

"I've been coming to the Stony Field Farm Stand since I was a boy," the fire captain told them. "This area just won't be the same without it."

"Thank you," Miriam replied. "You are very kind."

"It's the truth, ma'am," the fire captain said. "I'll wish you folks a good night, now."

After his departure, Miriam had gone back to the couch, slowly sinking down upon it. The farm stand was gone. Even if they did rebuild, a new one would never be the same. Its walls would contain no memories of Daed.

"You are tired and no wonder," Rachel said. "Let me put some *kaffi* on."

"I'll do it, Aenti Rachel," Leah said. She got to her feet and hurried out to the kitchen.

"I know we can rebuild," Miriam said, in answer to Daniel. "It's just . . ." Her voice broke. "The farm stand— *that* farm stand—has been there for so long. When I think of all Daed's hard work . . . he cared about it so."

"We all care about it," Bishop John said in his calm, quiet way. "I know there were some who were uncertain at first, but that was many years ago. I don't think there is one among us who would argue against the fact that the farm stand has brought great benefit to us all. I will have to speak to the deacons, of course. But I think I can say you will have the settlement's full support and assistance if you do decide to rebuild."

"*Danki*, John," Miriam said. She reached for Sarah's hand and held it fast. "We appreciate that."

Rat-a-tat-tat. There was a knock at the front door.

"I'll go," Amelia Brennemann said. "I'm closest."

She got up and went out into the hall. Miriam could hear a murmur of low voices. A moment later, Amelia returned, an *Englisch* man at her side. Miriam recognized him at once. It was Ernest Tompkins, who owned the lumberyard in town. Jacob and Ernest had been good friends. Ernest Tompkins had been among the *Englisch* mourners at her father's funeral, Miriam remembered, one of the first to offer his condolences.

"Good evening to you, Miriam, Daniel," he said. He turned, taking in the others in his greeting.

"Ernest," Daniel said. He rose to shake Ernest Tompkins's hand. "It is good of you to come."

"Sit down, please," Miriam said.

"No, no," Ernest Tompkins said, raising a hand to halt Miriam when she would have risen. "The last thing you need is a million visitors. I don't intend to stay long. I just wanted to say how sorry I am that the farm stand is gone. I remember when your father first decided to build it. We talked over the plans for quite some time."

Miriam and Sarah exchanged a glance. They had been too young when the stand was built to remember that, but they didn't doubt the man's words.

"I don't know what your intentions for the future are," Mr. Tompkins went on, "and maybe it's too soon for you to know yourselves."

"We were just discussing that," Miriam admitted.

"Well," Ernest Tompkins said, "that's fine. I just wanted you to know that, if you decide to rebuild, I hope you'll let

225

me help. Jacob Lapp was a fine man, and it was an honor to call him my friend. I wish I could say I can give you whatever you need, but in these hard times—"

"We'd never ask such a thing, Mr. Tompkins," Miriam exclaimed.

"I know that," he said with just the hint of a smile. "That doesn't mean I don't wish that I could make the offer. What I'm thinking is that we could share the load. You decide what you want to do, then let's sit down and talk it over, just like Jacob and I used to do. I'll get you the best deal I can on all your supplies. I drive a pretty mean bargain, if I do say so myself."

"That's very generous of you," Bishop John said.

"Jacob was a generous man," Ernest Tompkins replied as he turned in Bishop John's direction. "Some generosity in return seems only right. Call it a tribute, if you like."

He turned back to Miriam and Daniel. "If you do rebuild, you might consider getting that young Eli King to help. I've never seen anyone with such a good hand when it comes to wood, and that's a fact. I've been after him to bring me some things to sell at the store."

"What do you mean?" Miriam asked, curious.

"I mean, Eli's got the makings of a first-rate craftsman. He's been building chairs, tables, a cabinet that any cabinetmaker would be proud to call his own. That boy's got talent."

"Does he," Sarah said in a quiet, thoughtful voice.

"He does indeed," Mr. Tompkins assured her. "Well, I've said what I came to say and I won't trouble you any further. Good night, now."

"There'll be coffee in a minute," Miriam said, getting to her feet. "Leah's just now making some."

"No, thank you." Ernest Tompkins shook his head. "And don't stand on ceremony. I can see myself out."

"I'll go with you," Daniel's father said. He rose and accompanied Ernest Tompkins to the door. "Well," he said as he returned, "that was a welcome surprise."

"It was," Miriam agreed. She rubbed her forehead. "But I just don't know."

"You don't have to decide right this minute," Rachel remarked.

"Good!" Miriam said with a smile. "Oh, Leah," she went on as Leah came back into the room. "Thank you. That coffee smells so good. And you brought in the sandwiches. How thoughtful of you."

"I thought you might be hungry," Leah said. Carefully she set the heavy tray she'd prepared down on the coffee table in front of the couch. "Though I have to tell the truth," she said as she straightened up. "I thought you might be hungry because I was!"

"Then by all means let's eat something," Miriam said. "I'm sure that will make us all feel better."

The next few minutes were occupied by everyone getting something to eat. Daniel stayed close by Miriam's side.

"There is something I am wondering," he said. He paused to take a sip of coffee. "Though perhaps not. Maybe it is too soon to discuss something like this . . ."

"Gracious, Daniel!" Miriam exclaimed. "Now you're going to have to tell us. Otherwise we'll all die of curiosity."

"I'd prefer it if you did not do that," Daniel said.

227

"Thank you," Miriam answered. "I'd prefer not to do it myself."

Sarah choked on a sip of coffee. Quickly Miriam turned to thump her sister on the back.

"Sorry," Sarah said. "I think that sip went down the wrong way."

"What are you wondering about, Daniel?" his mother asked. "Tell us."

"I wonder if we should do more than just rebuild the farm stand," Daniel said. "Perhaps we should expand it."

"Expand it," Miriam echoed. "How?"

"By selling all sorts of other things!" Leah burst out. "Woodworking and quilts. I've always wanted to make quilts to sell. We could have a bigger refrigerator case for more food. The *Englischers* always want to know what we eat. Haven't you noticed that? I have. And I—"

"Why, Leah!" Rachel said.

Leah's face turned bright red. She clapped a hand across her mouth.

"No, let her go on," Daniel said with a smile. "I could not have put it better myself, though I would not have thought of the food."

"What Leah has been saying—is that what you meant?" Miriam asked, looking up at Daniel.

"It is," Daniel said. His blue eyes twinkled at Leah, whose hand remained firmly across her mouth. "I am wondering whether God has given us an opportunity rather than a disaster, painful as losing the old farm stand is."

"That is well spoken," Bishop John said.

"It is." Miriam nodded. She pulled in a deep breath and then smiled up at Daniel. "And thinking about what's happened that way already makes me feel better, I must admit." She turned to Sarah. "What do you think?"

"I agree with all of you," Sarah said. "Though contemplating how to plan it all makes my head swim."

"Fortunately we don't have to do it all tonight," Daniel said. "But if we are in agreement, then we can proceed." He turned to Bishop John. "Will you speak with the deacons?"

"I will." Bishop John nodded. "And I will also speak to Victor King. He should be told of Ernest Tompkins's praise of Eli."

"Ja," Daniel agreed. "I would like to see this woodwork of his." He looked at Miriam. "Perhaps that, too, could be sold at the new farm stand?"

"Perhaps," she said, smiling.

"And now I think we should say good night," Rachel said. She got to her feet. "And I think that Leah can take her hand down from her mouth so that she can say a proper good night as well."

"Good night," Leah said.

Miriam rose from the couch to give the young woman a hug. "I look forward to hearing all your ideas, Leah," she said. "And to seeing the quilts."

"I haven't made them yet," Leah confessed. "I just want to."

"Wanting to is a fine place to start," Miriam said. She gave Leah's shoulders a quick squeeze. "Thank you all for your support. I think that, with God's help, we will make this work."

* *

Late that night, Miriam and Daniel climbed the stairs to bed. The old farmhouse was still and silent all around them.

I love this house, Miriam thought as she followed the glow of the kerosene lamp that Daniel carried. He went into the bedroom, setting the lamp on the nightstand by his side of the bed. Miriam paused for a moment on the threshold.

"What is it?" Daniel asked.

"I'm not entirely sure," Miriam answered with a little laugh. "I was just thinking about how much I love this house. The way it feels so . . . enduring, even though it has known sadness."

"I know what you mean," Daniel said. "My parents' house feels the same way, as if it will withstand whatever comes."

"Whatever comes," Miriam echoed.

"Miriam," Daniel said softly. "Come to bed."

Slowly Miriam stepped across the threshold, crossing the room to Daniel like a moth drawn to a candle flame. Daniel turned and extinguished the light, but even in the dark, Miriam's course was unerring. She paused in front of him. Daniel's form was a dark outline against the window.

"There's a full moon tonight," Miriam whispered. "In all the excitement, I hadn't noticed."

"It's beautiful," Daniel said. With deft fingers, he removed Miriam's *kapp*, then went to work on the pins that held her hair tightly against her head. It fell down around her shoulders, cascading down her back in a thick stream of gold.

"As are you," Daniel whispered.

"Daniel," Miriam said. *"Daniel."*

And then there were no words for a very long time. Only the rush of blood, both quick and slow, and the sounding of two hearts, finally freed of all constraints, at long last beating as one.

Later, lying against the cool, crisp sheets, Miriam watched the moon streaming in through the window. She could see the outline of Daniel's shoulder as he slept, face toward the window just like always.

And then, in his sleep, Daniel turned, just as Miriam had always hoped and dreamed he would. One hand reached out, as if in search of her. Hardly daring to breathe, Miriam placed her own within it, saw and felt the way Daniel's fingers curved around hers. He shifted position yet again, moving closer, and pulled her into the circle of his arms.

Tears of joy flooded Miriam's eyes. But she did not let them fall. Instead, she laid her head upon her husband's chest, closed her eyes, and slept a sleep without dreams until the first light of morning.

Seventeen

The weeks that followed were some of the busiest Miriam could ever remember. The August days were hot and fine. For Miriam, every day was about rebuilding the farm stand. In the days that followed the fire, she and Daniel and Sarah, along with Daniel's brothers, removed the debris from the land. It was painful to think that so little was left of what Daed had built with his own hands, and yet Miriam felt excited about what was to come.

After supper each evening, Miriam and Sarah cleared the table and then covered it with a big piece of white butcher paper Sarah had bought in town. Then Sarah, Miriam, and Daniel did what Sarah called brainstorming. Making sketches and jotting down their ideas for what the new farm stand should be, no matter how seemingly unrealistic or far-flung. The idea was not to rule anything out, Sarah said, to let your imagination soar.

Then came two weekends when everyone in the district, it seemed, came together to build the new stand. Miriam felt a thrill as she watched the framing go up, and then the walls and roof and doors.

She could not imagine how she could be any happier with the end result. Where once the farm stand had consisted of one building, now there were two, side by side, built by her neighbors on two successive weekends with the supplies Daniel and Ernest Tompkins had negotiated. The larger building would be much like the farm stand that Jacob had created: a place to sell seasonal produce along with pickles, preserves, and pies. But right beside it, like a younger sibling, was a smaller building that would be primarily devoted to other kinds of handmade Plain goods.

There would be racks to display quilts. Carved wooden shelves that would be for sale at the same time they displayed homemade preserves. There would even be Plain clothing for sale to tourists. And, like the produce stand, the new building would have a special set of refrigerators, freezers, and display cases for some of the food items that so interested the *Englischers*, so that an *Englisch* family could have a real "Amish" meal right in their very own home.

This last idea was Miriam's brainstorm, though part of the credit certainly went to Leah as well. It was a big risk, Miriam thought now, as she stood inside the main farm stand. But sometimes the only way to create change was to take a chance. Hadn't she just learned that for herself, in other areas of her life?

She turned a slow circle, gazing around the bright, clean space. She breathed in deeply, savoring the new-wood smell. There was so much room now! New front doors that slid open almost silently on their tracks, tucking away inside specially built pockets that Eli and Daniel had designed. Daniel had taken Ernest Tompkins's words to heart, asking Eli to build all the new shelves, both freestanding and along the walls. Eli had gone to work with a will, getting the shelves up in record time.

But he had showed his dedication long before that, within a week of the original farm stand's destruction. Miriam, Sarah, and Daniel had been in the kitchen one night after supper when there had come a knock at the kitchen door. It was Victor and Eli. Victor King's wagon stood in the side yard. In it were two new display tables, ready to be put to use at once. Eli had worked on them in the evenings all week long.

The thoughtfulness of Eli's gesture, to say nothing of his hard work, still brought tears to Miriam's eyes. If Miriam had entertained any doubts about keeping the stand going, Eli's dedication had put them to rest. Thanks to his hard work, and the second "stand raising" the previous weekend, the farm stand would officially reopen for business on Monday morning.

Where are the tables? Miriam suddenly wondered. Surely they ought to be inside. Could Eli be working on them next door? Although the frame for the second building was in place, the interior was still being finished. This had seemed the sensible course. That way, the produce stand could get back in business while the finishing touches were put on the craft space. Then, when the weather grew colder, the main section of the farm stand would close and the smaller building would open. During the winter the smaller space would be much more manageable to heat. For the time being, at Daniel's suggestion, Eli was using the second building as a carpentry workshop.

I'll just stop in there on my way back to the house, Miriam thought. There was really nothing for her to do here at the moment. She just hadn't been able to resist the impulse to stroll down to the farm stand on such a beautiful day, particularly since she was on her own. Daniel and most of the other men were away at the horse auction. Sarah had no interest in attending the show, but she had accepted a ride into town. She had asked if Miriam wanted to come along, but Miriam had declined. A quiet afternoon on her own had sounded perfect.

She turned to go. She took a step toward the back door of the farm stand, then stopped as, abruptly, the room began to spin around her. Miriam made a distressed sound. She tried to take another step, but her legs refused to cooperate. Her knees gave way and she crumpled to the floor; she remembered nothing more.

"What do you think?" Eli asked.

As Leah watched, he lifted one of the two produce display tables up by handholds he'd just finished carving underneath the tabletop. Then he took several steps. The table slid forward easily on the two sturdy wheels that were now affixed to the legs at the far end. Eli set the table down. He walked to the wheels and toed the locking mechanism down into position. Now the table would stay right where he'd put it.

"It's perfect!" Leah cried. She did her best not to clap her hands in delight, then gave in and did it anyhow. "Sort of like the world's biggest cart!"

"Something like that," Eli said with a quick smile. He took a step back, surveying his handiwork. "You really think Miriam will like it?"

"No," Leah said, then bit her tongue to hold back a laugh at Eli's stricken expression. "I don't *think*, Eli. I *know*. She'll never drop one of those table legs on her foot again. Not only that, one person can easily move the tables wherever they need to go. Think how much time we'll save getting set up every morning and putting everything away at night."

"I was thinking of that," Eli admitted. "I just wish I'd thought of it sooner. That way, I could have built them like this from the start. These tables are my second version."

"Well, you have made it right, now," Leah said simply. "That will be enough."

Eli's head swiveled toward her, an expression Leah couldn't quite decipher in his green eyes.

"You think it is so easy to correct a mistake?" he asked.

Leah sucked in a breath to make a quick response, then hesitated. Somehow she didn't think Eli was talking about display tables anymore. She released her breath slowly before she spoke.

"Not always, no." All of a sudden, she smiled. "If my

aenti Rachel were here, I'm almost certain she'd say that it's the mistakes that are the hardest to fix that are the ones we need to fix most of all."

"You like living with your *aenti* and *onkel*, don't you?" Eli began to put his tools away, carefully stowing them in the toolbox.

"Oh, *ja*," Leah said at once. "But then, it's all I've ever known. I don't really remember my parents. I was so young when they died. How are things with Victor?"

"Gut," Eli replied. "Better than when I first arrived. What Mr. Tompkins said . . . and Daniel showing his faith in me by asking me to help rebuild the farm stand . . . those things helped a lot. Still . . ." He broke off and was silent for so long that Leah thought he wasn't going to continue. "I am sorry to have disappointed Victor," Eli said at last. "My mistake is a big one to correct."

"But you are working on it," Leah said quietly.

"Ja," Eli said. "I am."

"Then if your brother is as fair as you say he is, he will see that."

"I hope he does," Eli said.

He continued to hold Leah's gaze. The silence stretched out. Not uncomfortable, but not quite comfortable, either, Leah thought.

"It's getting late," she said. "I should get home. I promised Aenti Rachel I would get supper started. She went into town to do some shopping while Onkel John is at the horse auction."

"Ja," Eli replied. "I must get home also." He fastened the lid on the toolbox, then stowed it on the workbench he'd

set up in one corner. "I will come early tomorrow and put the wheels on the other table. Then we can wheel them over."

"That sounds good."

Together they left the building. Leah noted the way Eli held the door for her before locking it carefully behind him. He was taking the new responsibilities Daniel and Miriam had given him very seriously. *He will make no mistakes with this,* Leah thought.

"That's odd," she suddenly said.

"What?"

"The back door to the farm stand is open."

"It's probably just Sarah or Miriam," Eli said.

"It cannot be Sarah," Leah told him. "She went into town with Aenti Rachel. But you're right. It's probably just Miriam."

"Do you want to take a look?"

"I do." Leah nodded, grateful that he understood. "I don't mean to sound silly, it's just—"

"It's just that everything is so new," Eli filled in. "You don't want anything to happen."

With Leah in the lead, the two walked the short distance between the two buildings. But as they approached the open doorway, Eli stepped in front of her. Leah opened her mouth to protest, then closed it with a snap. If there *was* danger, he would face it first.

Leah held her breath as Eli eased his head in through the open door.

"Leah," he said. Just the two syllables of her name. But they made Leah's blood run cold. Eli stepped inside the farm stand, pulling her with him.

239

Miriam lay in a crumpled heap on the floor.

With a cry of dismay, Leah darted forward to kneel at Miriam's side. Her fingers trembled as she searched for a pulse. She found it, but it seemed to Leah that Miriam's heart was beating far too fast, though maybe it was just her own.

"Miriam?" she asked. "Can you tell me what happened?"

But Miriam did not answer or open her eyes.

"Is she—" Eli began.

"She's alive," Leah said. "Her heart is beating. I think she'll be all right." She twisted her head to gaze up at Eli. "Do you know where the Kauffmans live?"

"Ja." Eli nodded. He crouched down beside Leah. "What about them?"

"Ruth Kauffman is our *dokterfraa.* You must go to my *aenti* and *onkel's* house, take the horse and buggy, and go and fetch Ruth Kauffman. Will you do that?"

"Ja." Eli hesitated for just a moment, then he said, "But I thought your *aenti* went into town."

"She did," Rachel said. "But she and Sarah took Miriam and Daniel's horse and buggy. Ours are in the barn at home."

"I will be quick," Eli promised. "Try not to worry."

"I will do my best," Leah said. *"Danki,* Eli."

He reached to grip her shoulder tightly, and then he was gone. Leah knelt beside Miriam, praying as she had never prayed before.

Please, God, she thought. Let the words she'd spoken to Eli be true. *Let Miriam be all right.*

Eighteen

Miriam opened her eyes. The world around her swam slowly into view. She blinked for a moment and closed them again. She was in her own bed, in her own bedroom. Late afternoon sunlight streamed in through the window. The last thing she remembered was being in the farm stand, thinking about having to heat only the smaller building in the winter. How much time had passed since then? She turned her head and saw Daniel sitting in the bedroom chair, watching her with concern.

"Daniel?" she asked softly.

"*Ja*, Miriam. I am here," Daniel said.

"But," Miriam protested, "the horse auction."

The bed dipped as Daniel sat down upon it. "Miriam," he said, and even through the fog that still seemed to envelop her Miriam thought she could hear both the love and exasperation in her husband's voice. "I think that you are more important than some old horse auction. Besides . . ." Gently Daniel captured one of her hands, covered it with both his own. "I was already on my way home."

As if from a great distance, Miriam heard the sound of her own laughter, marveled at the gentle, loving sound.

"Ah!" The door to the bedroom opened and the *dokter-fraa*, Ruth Kauffman, stuck her head in. "I gather she is awake and feeling better."

"I think so," Daniel answered with a smile.

"Oh, Ruth. I did not know that Daniel sent for you," Miriam said. She began to push herself upright but Daniel pressed her back onto the pillows with a gentle hand on her shoulder. "I am sorry to be so much trouble."

"It is no trouble," the *dokterfraa* said simply. "And it wasn't Daniel, it was Leah Gingerich and Eli King. They are the ones who found you this morning. You have been sleeping now for hours."

"What?" Miriam lifted her free hand to rub her forehead. "I'm sorry. I guess I don't remember . . . Am I ill? Is something wrong with me?"

"Not a thing," Ruth said. "As a matter of fact, unless I am very much mistaken, a great deal is well."

"Then why . . ." Miriam began. All of a sudden, she caught her breath. She looked up into Daniel's face. Never, or so it seemed to her, had she seen it so suffused with joy. A great and terrible hope bloomed in Miriam's heart.

"I am . . . that is, could I be . . ."

"Pregnant?" the *dokterfraa* said. "I believe so, yes. I must ask, have you missed any of your courses recently?"

"They've been irregular," Miriam answered, slightly embarrassed to be discussing women's matters like this in front of her husband.

Ruth nodded. "You must also see an *Englischer* doctor this week, to be certain, and also to make sure there are no problems. You did pass out, *ja?* But to my eyes, all the signs are there, and I can see nothing wrong with you at the moment."

"A baby," Miriam whispered, placing her hand over her belly. "After so long."

"Your mother took a long time to conceive, also, as I recall," Ruth said. "But it seems for you, as for her, God has many gifts to bestow."

Miriam brought Daniel's hand to her cheek. *"Ja,"* she said softly. "I know He does."

"Well," Ruth said, "I will leave the two of you alone now. See that she rests today, Daniel."

"I will," Daniel promised.

The *dokterfraa* left the room, closing the door quietly behind her.

"Oh, Daniel, I can hardly believe it!" Miriam said. "A baby! Why now after all this time?"

"God has a reason for everything," Daniel said. "For myself, I do not need to know why. All I want to do is to give thanks."

"Ja," Miriam said. "And so do I."

This time when she moved to sit upright, Daniel did not

stop her. Instead, he moved over so that they sat side by side, and he took her hand in his. Her heart as full of joy as she could ever remember it being, Miriam bowed her head along with Daniel as they thanked God for all the gifts He had already bestowed upon them, and all the ones that were yet to come.

Nineteen

A baby!" Leah cried. "Oh, but that's wonderful!"

"It is," Aenti Rachel agreed. "But, Leah, it is not our way to speak so openly about a woman with child when it is still so early. It is only because you and Eli found Miriam when she was unconscious that so many of us are here now—and know the good news."

"*Ja*, Aenti, I understand," Leah said. "I must be very patient and not tell anyone else."

"Sometimes seeing God's work takes patience," Bishop John said. "Miriam and Daniel have waited a long time."

The three were gathered in the farmhouse kitchen, along with Daniel's parents, Sarah, and Victor and Eli King. Amelia Brennemann had made coffee and brought out some of Miriam's homemade rolls while they waited for news of her health. Ruth Kauffman had just gone home, after assuring them that Miriam was resting comfortably. It was Daniel who had told them the glad tidings, when he came down from the bedroom to thank Leah and Eli.

Bishop John cleared his throat. "Eli, I must speak of a matter that involves you."

"No, Onkel John," Leah said at once, then she flushed as she became the focus of all eyes. She took a quick breath, willing her voice to remain steady. "I know Eli wasn't supposed to drive. But it was an emergency. Surely he should not be punished for that. But if you decide he must be punished, then you must punish me as well. I was the one who asked him to take the horse and buggy and go for the *dokterfraa*."

"Which we are very grateful for," Sarah said quickly.

Bishop John didn't seem to notice Sarah's comment. He was focused on his niece. "Thank you, Leah," he said. "But I have no intention of punishing Eli. In fact, I think there has been quite enough of that." Bishop John switched his attention to Eli himself, standing silently beside his older brother. "Wouldn't you agree, Eli?"

Eli's eyes grew wide. "It is not a matter for me to decide," he replied.

"John," said Victor quietly, "may we know what you are talking about?"

"A number of days ago, I received a letter," Bishop John explained. "It was from Isaac Wittmer, who is the bishop of the district in Ohio where Eli's mother lives. In it, he tells me that you weren't driving the buggy when it crashed that day, Eli. Instead, it was his son, Reuben. Is this true?"

"*Ja.* It is true," Eli said softly.

"What do you mean it's true?" Leah burst out before she could stop herself. "All these months you've been letting people believe you did something wrong!"

"I did do something wrong," Eli replied. "I did not drive the buggy, it is true, but I didn't stop the race, either."

"That still does not tell me why you did not tell the truth," the bishop said.

"I wasn't trying to tell a lie," Eli said quickly. "I just thought perhaps it was not my truth to tell. If I spoke, then Reuben never would, and it seemed to me that it was important that he make his own peace with God. If he could do that . . ." Eli's voice trailed off.

"*Danki*, Eli," Bishop John said. "I think that I have heard enough. I must speak to the deacons, of course, but I will give them my recommendation that your punishment be lifted. You may have made an error in judgment when you took part in a buggy race, but since then I think your behavior has been beyond reproach."

Leah tried not to smile as she saw Eli blush at her *onkel*'s words.

"I am proud to have you as a member of our community," Bishop John went on. "But Bishop Isaac writes that, now that they know the truth, there are many in your settlement who would like to welcome you back to Ohio."

Eli's eyes shot to Leah's face, then dropped. "I would like to speak with my mother first, if I may. And to Victor, also."

"You must take all the time you need, Eli," said Bishop John. He got to his feet. "I think that now that we know Miriam is well, perhaps it is time for all of us to go home."

247

"I will look in tomorrow if I may," Rachel said as she, too, rose. "I don't imagine Miriam will want to stay in bed for long."

"I think you are right about that!" Sarah answered with a laugh. "Let me walk you out."

"We'll go, too," Amelia said. "Martin, don't you think now would be a fine time to talk to Victor about that matter you wished to discuss?"

"What?" Martin asked. "Oh, *ja*, of course. Victor, I've been meaning to ask you . . ."

Seizing Eli's brother by the arm, he marched him out the kitchen door. In the space of no more than a moment, Leah and Eli were left alone.

He stood across the table from Leah, arms loosely at his sides. For the first and only time since they had met, it seemed to Leah that Eli was at a loss. He would not meet her eyes.

"What will you do?" she asked. "Will you stay or go?"

"That depends," Eli said.

Leah felt a familiar spurt of irritation. What was it about Eli, she wondered, that got under her skin so? He'd done it from the day they'd first met.

"Well, of course it *depends*," she said tartly. "The question is, on what?"

Eli smiled. He lifted his head and looked Leah straight in the eye. "On whether or not I have a good enough reason to stay, of course."

Leah's heart began to pound. "What kind of a reason?" she asked.

"If I have to tell you, that settles it," Eli answered. "I'm going back to Ohio."

"I wish you wouldn't," Leah said.

"How much do you wish it?" Eli asked.

Leah put her hands on her hips. She was trying to look severe, but she was unable to hold back a smile. It seemed Eli wasn't the only one who could get underneath somebody's skin.

"Eli King," she said, "that's enough. If you want to know more, you'll just have to be patient."

"I can do that," Eli said. He flashed that grin that Leah used to find so wicked but that now filled her heart with joy. "And do you know what else I can do? Soon I will be able to drive a courting buggy, won't I?"

Now Leah was the one who smiled.

Twenty

T wins!" Miriam exclaimed. She gazed at the *Englisch* doctor in astonishment. Her hand reached out for Daniel's, silently seeking support. She felt him grasp her fingers, thread his own through them, and hold on tight. "Twins? You are sure?"

"As sure as I can be at this stage of the pregnancy," Dr. Harrington said with a smile.

At Ruth Kauffman's insistence, Miriam had made an appointment to see an *Englisch* doctor in town. Annaliese had been a patient of Dr. Harrington's during her first pregnancy. The doctor was an older woman who was trusted and well liked within the Plain community.

"Twins," Miriam said once more. "After all this time?"

"God has given us a very special gift." Daniel spoke quietly.

"Ja," Miriam answered swiftly. She gave his hand a squeeze. "That is so."

"Is there anything special we need to know or do?" Daniel asked Dr. Harrington. "This fainting, will it happen again?"

"I don't think so. But I do think you need to be sensible about the amount of work you do, Miriam. I know it's too much to ask a Plain woman to sit down and put her feet up . . ."

Miriam smiled.

"But it may come to that as the months go along. Why don't you come back and see me in . . ." The doctor consulted a laptop computer. "About three weeks' time. Though of course you should call if you have any questions or concerns. You have a phone at the farm stand, don't you?"

"No," Miriam replied. "But Daniel's parents have a pay phone in their barn."

The doctor frowned. "It's just a precaution, but considering that you are pregnant with twins, it might be a good time to put a phone in at the farm stand. And not a pay phone. If anything should go wrong, you'll want to summon help quickly."

"We'll do that," Daniel said at once, to Miriam's surprise.

Miriam considered the doctor with curiosity. "You come to the stand?" She didn't remember seeing her, but then, so many *Englischers* came and went.

"Oh, yes," Dr. Harrington said with a smile. "Your father and I were old friends. He always saved me a jar of your rose hip jelly."

"Then we will continue the tradition," Miriam promised.

"Thank you. I would like that," Dr. Harrington replied. "Any more questions?"

Miriam exchanged a look with Daniel. "I don't think so," she said. "At least, not now."

"You feel free to call me if you change your mind," the doctor said. She got to her feet. Miriam and Daniel did the same. "Congratulations, folks. I'll look forward to helping you welcome a new generation into your home."

"Twins!" Sarah said. She caught Miriam by both hands and twirled her around in a great circle.

"Stop!" Miriam protested, laughing. "I already feel dizzy enough!"

"Twins," Sarah said. She collapsed onto the couch, pulling Miriam down beside her. "I can't believe it!"

Miriam laughed. "That's exactly how I felt."

"What will you call them?" Sarah asked. "Have you decided?"

"Give us some time," Daniel protested. "We only just found out."

"And we don't even know if we're having girls or boys yet," Miriam added.

"It could be one of each," Sarah remarked. "But I know you, Miriam. You probably had half a dozen names for each picked out on the way home."

"Well," Miriam began.

"I knew it!" Sarah cried.

"We did have a few thoughts. Edna for certain, if God gives us a girl."

"Oh," Sarah said. "Just like Mamm. And if there's a boy?"

"Daniel," Miriam said softly. She looked up at Daniel, who stood, quiet and steady as always, just inside the living room door. "I have always dreamed of having a son to name for his father."

"That's it. It's official," Sarah announced. "I am going to cry."

One week later, Miriam and Daniel stood in the Philadelphia airport, watching Sarah's great, silver plane lift off into the sky. Though Sarah had insisted she could get to the airport on her own, Miriam had been equally insistent: She would see her sister off. And when Sarah returned once the babies were born, as she promised to do, this time Miriam knew just how she would feel. She would welcome her sister with an open heart and open arms.

"It was a good visit, in the end, wasn't it?" Daniel asked quietly.

"Ja." Miriam nodded. "It was." She turned from the window with its view of planes lifting off and touching down. "But I am ready to be out of the hustle and bustle of this *Englisch* world she has chosen."

"Then come," Daniel said. He extended one hand and Miriam took it. "Let us go home."

Miriam Brennemann's
Blackberry Jam

Miriam makes her blackberry jam by the "slow cook" method her mother, Edna, learned from her mother. Edna Lapp wrote the technique down in a book that Miriam treasures (and uses) to this day.

In spite of its name, this method really isn't all that slow. It will produce a slightly softer jam than one made with commercial pectin. But Miriam thinks the flavor is much better because the fruit-to-sugar ratio is higher on the fruit side. Her Stony Field Farm Stand customers seem to agree! This blackberry jam is always one of the stand's bestsellers.

4 cups fresh blackberries
3 cups granulated sugar, divided into three portions
    of 1 cup each
½ large, tart apple, such as Granny Smith

Rinse the berries in cold water. Put the berries through a food mill or a strainer to remove most of the seeds.

Pour the slightly thick and frothy juice/pulp mixture into a large, heavy-bottomed pot. (Miriam uses her mother's enameled Dutch oven.)

Add the first cup of sugar to the mixture and stir to dissolve.

Cut the half apple into four slices. Remove the core, but leave the skin on. Place the slices in the pot.

Set the burner to medium, and heat the mixture, stirring occasionally, until it reaches a rolling boil. A rolling boil is a boil that cannot be stirred down, so you will want to stir more as the mixture begins to boil to make sure that the rolling boil point has been reached (and also to make sure the mixture doesn't burn or stick to the bottom of the pot).

Once the mixture reaches the rolling boil stage, set a timer for five minutes. Continue to stir, adjusting the temperature if you feel you need to, until the timer goes off.

At the end of five minutes, add the second cup of sugar and stir to dissolve. Continue to stir as the mixture returns to a rolling boil. Set another five minutes on the timer. Stir for this five minutes, then add the final cup of sugar when the timer goes off.

Repeat the stirring/reaching rolling boil stage one last time. (The amount of time it takes the berry mixture to return to a rolling boil grows shorter and shorter as you go along.)

At the end of the final five minutes, take the pan off the heat. Remove the apple slices. (They make a tasty sweet snack when cool.)

Ladle the hot jam into the size of jars you like. Miriam prefers the eight-ounce size. Prepare jars for water bath according to the manufacturer's instructions. This recipe makes approximately four eight-ounce jars.

If Miriam has jam left over, she puts it in a little dish and saves it for her family to use immediately.

Glossary

ab in kopp   crazy

ach   oh

aenti   aunt

Ausbund   hymn book

blabbermaul   chatterbox; blabbermouth

boppli (plural: bopplin)   baby

daed, daedi   dad, daddy

danki   thank you

dawdi-haus   grandparents' house attached to main house

Deitsch   Pennsylvania German

dochder (plural: dochdern)   daughter

dokterfraa   a woman healer

dumm   dumb; stupid

Englisch   non-Amish

Englischer   non-Amish person

fraa   wife

gennuk   enough

graabhof   graveyard

gross-mammi   grandma

gude mariye   good morning

gut   good

gut nacht   good night

ich liebe dich   I love you

ja   yes

kaffi   coffee

kapp   prayer head covering for females

kind (plural: kinder)   child

komm   come

Leit   the people, the district

maedel (plural: maedels)   girl; young unmarried woman

mamm   mom

mei kinder   my children

mutza   coat worn by a man to Sunday services

onkel   uncle

Ordnung   district's rules of behavior and worship

rumspringa   running-around time before baptism

schatzi   little treasure (an endearment)

Schteckliman   intermediary between groom's and bride's
parents

snitz pie   dried apple pie

sohn (plural: söhne)   son

vorsinger   lead singer at services or singings

was iss letz?   what's wrong?
wie geht's?   hello, how are you doing?
wilkomm   welcome
wunderbaar   wonderful
yunga   young one

If you enjoyed *Summer Promise*, don't miss

AUTUMN GRACE

the second book in the Amish Seasons series,
available now!

Ready to find
your next great read?

Let us help.

Visit prh.com/nextread

Penguin
Random
House